legant, precision... *Guardian*

'Arresting . . . Godden's free association approach is a defining, animating force'
Daily Mail

'What a writer. What a novel. The inventiveness of this use of story and form to delve in and out of loss, grief but, ultimately, hope and friendship had me hooked until the last page'
Travis Alabanza

'One of the most brilliant, incisive, incredibly inspirational writers I've ever come across'
Andi Oliver, Sky Arts Book Club

'Highly original . . . This lyrical tale asks potent questions about class, race, gender while examining society's fraught and often complex relationship with mortality'
Cosmopolitan

'Timeless, brave and beautiful. This is a book for everyone who understands they hang suspended between the click and the bang'
John Higgs

'A beguiling book and one which is almost too easy to devour . . . An irresistible novel which speaks equally to the act of living as it does to the inevitability of dying'

MRS DEATH MISSES DEATH

SALENA GODDEN

CANONGATE

This paperback edition published in Great Britain in 2022
by Canongate Books

First published in Great Britain in 2021 by Canongate Books Ltd,
14 High Street, Edinburgh EH1 1TE

canongate.co.uk

2

British Library Cataloguing-in-Publication Data
A catalogue record for this book is available on
request from the British Library

ISBN 978 1 83885 122 4

Typeset in Centaur MT by Palimpsest Book Production Ltd,
Falkirk, Stirlingshire

Printed and bound in Great Britain by Clays Ltd, Elcograf S.p.A.

Mourn the dead and fight like hell for the living

Disclaimer:

This book contains dead people.

This book cannot see the future. This book is dabbling in the past. This book is not about funerals although funerals are mentioned. You do not have to wear black to read this work. You do not have to bring flowers.

Caution: This work contains traces of eulogy.

Warning: This work contains violent deaths.

Spoiler alert: We will all die in the end.

This book cannot change the ending or your ending or its own ending. This book does not know how to switch on the light at the end of the tunnel. This book cannot contact the other side. This book cannot speak to the dead or for the dead. This book will not confirm if there is an afterlife or an alternative universe. This book will not improve your karma. This book will not nag you to live a healthier life. This book will not help you quit smoking. This book is not going to urge you to age gracefully. This book does not advocate the use of that funereal phrase 'he had a good innings'. This book does not contain any person or persons clapping their hands and singing *kum-by-yah-mi-lord*. This book may be used for mild to moderate relief from grief, fear and pain, however if symptoms persist please buy a ticket to see a live reading of this work where you will *find the others.*

Caution: Do not exceed death.

This work has a very high dead and death count. Take with caution. Take your time. Do your lifetime in your own life time. If you are sensitive or allergic to talk of the dead or non-living things use this work in small doses. This is not a self-help brochure. This is not a guide to avoiding dying. If you think you are about to drop dead, please seek medical advice immediately.

This work has very little to do with God, the Gods, Goddesses, Satan or the Devil. This work is not focused on a battle of good and evil or right and wrong. This is not about morality or heaven and hell or sinners and saints. This book does not judge you or your choices. This book is not connected to or promoting any religion or cult. This is not a map to the way out of here. This is not a compass. This book does not contain directions to heaven or hell – see also Elysium, Valhalla, Gan Eden, The Fields of Aaru, Vaikuntha, Tír na nÓg, Cockaigne, Big Rock Candy Mountain or any other world versions of otherworld.

This work calls the righteous spirits of all of our mighty ancestors now and in the hour of our need. We take a breath and look back in amazement and wonder at how our ancestors survived so we may also survive. We take another deep breath, we feel our hearts beating inside our bodies, and we celebrate that the same empowerment and spirit runs in our blood now and can be found in our DNA today. We give thanks to our ancestors, thanks for giving us life, for being alive to feel alive and to share this one magnificent connection to life and all living things.

This book does not mention every person that has ever died – if you wished this book to have mentioned another death, we can only apologise now in advance, for not knowing which death or dead celebrity you wanted mentioned and celebrated in this book at time of writing and printing. At the time of writing this book mourns for Prince, David Bowie, Leonard Cohen, Toni Morrison and Aretha Franklin. And this book sincerely hopes there aren't any more inspirational human beings, bold souls, brave hearts and superheroes to add to that dead list before we go to print. Amen.

This book contains traces of ghosts. This book may contain bones and other human remains. This book has been haunting me. This book may haunt you. This book is about you and me and all of us. We will use the term 'human' or 'human being' to mean people who identify as human, that is being 'alive' and 'living', and furthermore discuss how they are now 'dead' and use the word 'dead' to mean that the heart stopped beating and the brain ceased functioning and they are not breathing any more. This work does not contain zombies but has no prejudices against those that choose to be living dead.

This book knows loss and feels your pain. This book shares your fears and anxieties. This book will explore the worst-case scenarios. This book is afraid of death, but not afraid to speak about it. This book is in mourning and trying to understand this process of grieving. This book sends you all its love. This book says it's alright to cry on its shoulder.

This book is short because life is short. The time it took for us to evolve from *Homo sapiens* to modern civilisation, from the first cave paintings and words and stories and songs to the first book and the first bookshop, is a wonder and also relatively short. Any book with the word Death in the title must be light enough to carry in your hand luggage. It must be short enough to be read cover to cover on a train up from London to Liverpool. It must be loud enough to read during the length of a good belter of a thunderstorm, then when the storm passes and the clouds clear and the skies open up, the train doors open, and so will your heart.

These are the collected memoirs of Mrs Death, edited and compiled by me, Wolf Willeford. I'm a poet and I live in the attic rooms of the Forest Tavern in East London. Contained here are some of Mrs Death's private diary entries, some stories, poems and pieces of conversations I have had with Mrs Death; she who is Death, the woman who is the boss at the end of all of us. I share this hoping that it is the beginning of your own conversation with yourself and with your own precious time here.

When writing this I found that when people die, we write about them differently; it is as though we can speak freely; it is as though they have left the room. When writing about Death you soon realise it isn't all about Death and that you write about Life and the living: this is what I have learned whilst creating this work for you. This is a work of both fiction and non-fiction, a work of dreams and nightmares. Some names, dates and details have been changed to protect the living and amuse the dead.

This book is a matter of Life and Death.

Mrs Death's Diaries:
The First Morning of the First Mourning

Present day

When I called for change, did you pass by me? Did you see me today?

I sit on a bench outside London's King's Cross station. I like train stations and airports best. I like to sit in places where people come and go. I sit and watch you come and go, you say, goodbye and hello, come and go, goodbye and hello. It's as though you are not connected to each other. Goodbye, you say, clinging on to that last glance, you give a funny little wave. You don't know that you don't have to touch to touch, to see, to feel each other. Human beings were designed to be in contact without being in contact, to communicate without words, to call each other to each others' minds. Humans still have so much to learn about connection. But when you are in transition and whilst travelling you are tuned in to this, you are alive and alert. When you travel you wake up. You're awake and aware of changes, differences and sameness, strangers and each other. In transit you are occupied by Time and Space, by clocks and miles, by separation and reunion, your chance and your fate. Humans were built to travel, humans were made to move, to share and to migrate, just like butterflies and birds.

The history and the geography of human migration is nothing less than phenomenal.

The greatest trick man played was making you believe I was a man. They erased me and made you all believe that Death was male in spirit – the Grim Reaper in a black hood with a scythe. Remarkable that nobody questioned it really, don't you think? For surely only she who bears it, she who gave you life, can be she who has the power to take it. The one is she. And only she who is invisible can do the work of Death. And there is no human more invisible, more readily talked over, ignored, betrayed and easy to walk past than a woman; than a poor old black woman, a homeless black beggar-woman with knotty natty hair, broken back, walking ever so slow, slow, slow, pushing a shopping trolley full of plastic bottles.

Death is plastic, plastic is death.

When this all began, or when I began, was when life began, and that was when death began. Death is a bitch, Life is a bitch, but it's in poor taste to speak ill of the living. My sister cannot help herself but be Life and living and lively. LIFE! Oh she is abundant and demanding of all of our attentions. My sister is an over-achiever, laying eggs and fertilising life, shitting life everywhere, muck-spreading fertile life. Life shits life! Life is life everywhere!

I remember when this earth world was once a rock and a cold and dark place. I was there, we were there. I can recall the terrible smell of eggs; that's the main thing I remember, the stench. My sister is stinky. Death may stink of Death and of rot and decay but Life stinks too. Life and birth was always about eggs and shit. Volcanic. Sulphur. Fertiliser. Farts. The vagina awakes, yawns, stretches and burps and there we have blood, and from blood is life and love. And where there was blood there was life, and where there was life there was love, and where there was love there was life, and where there was life there was blood and where there was blood there was death. Around and around it goes, life and blood and love and death and time and space, around and around we go, spinning on this pretty blue rock in space we call planet earth.

Fish grew legs. Birds grew wings. Monkeys walked upright and tall. And that's when things got interesting for me. Because then came the first fires and the first stories, the first poets and the first songs, the first paintings on cave walls, daubed in ash and charcoal. Life and Death, we sisters, sat side by side together and warmed ourselves by the very first fires, with the first souls dancing in the first firelight, the first handprints, stickman images of their own selves on the walls of the caves. These were the first mirrors, man capturing man's own image. The smoke rising, the charcoal pictures telling us stories of life and death, long tall tales of hunts and kills, boasted of around the fire and scratched into the cave walls. And what do they tell us? What does the painter ask us with these cave paintings? Why, surely just variations of the same questions that painters and poets have always asked us over the centuries: *Who am I? Why am I? What is life? What is death? Can you see me? Will you hear this? Do you feel me?*

I am she and she is here. I see you. I hear you. I was always here, there and everywhere. Here was I and I am I and I am she. And you might want to ask me this:

Mrs Death, who was the first person to ever die?

OK. Let us picture that first morning of the first mourning.

That first longing, that first grief, the first heavy silence, the first missing shape, the spare fur in the circle in the cave, the first empty seat by the fire. The first time a human being grieved for another human being: the missed voice, the terrible pain, ache and longing, and there we have it, the first morning of the first mourning. And you, you're only human. Mankind. Womankind. You only have one job:

Be kind.

Kin.

You mark your place in time. You tell your tale. Time is short, a life is fast, but this picture on this cave wall may last longer than you will. You live forever in your words, in hearts and memories, in your creations and connections. The seeds you sow, the child you raise, the song you sing, the story you write with your time here. You are eternal, you are forever present in your oily DNA and your unique thumb print. You know you live now and here are all your fears: all your fears are here. And above all things you all fear, you fear me, you fear the end, you fear dancing with me, you fear Mrs Death.

Here is your proof, your evidence, the evidence you lived the life you lived, here in this time, in these words, in this story, in this song, in this painting. It is human nature to try to stop time, to try to capture a life, a shooting star, to pin the butterfly wings and snap the lid shut.

What do you have there in that box? *Look*, you say, *I have captured time, I have trapped a moment. Here I have my lifetime documented, a timeline made palpable, digestible, linear. Here I was born and I did grow teeth. Here I did love, and here were my tribe, my family, my loves and my loves lost. Here was my toil and struggle, my monsters, my Gods, my triumph and failure and passion. And here is my end, here my last thrill, my dance with you, Mrs Death.*

With me?
Yes, with you.
Let us dance, dance, dance.

Mrs Death: The First Mourning

Mrs Death sings:

the first fires, the first fires
the first morning of the first mourning
the first shape of the first loss

the first fires, the first fires
the first birth, the first blood
the first kill, the first blood spill

you're only human
you're only womankind
you're only human being
you're only mankind, be kind

the first sunrise, the first sunset
you're only human, you're only woman
you're only man, human, be kind
human being kind human being

the first stars in the first skies
the first stars in the first skies
you're only human, human being
be kind

the first cave, the first cave painting
the first word, the first art, the first heartbreak
the first morning of the first mourning
the first loss, the first blood, the first war

you're only human, you're only woman
you're only human, you're only man
you're only human, human being
humankind
be kind

Wolf: The First Time I Met Mrs Death

Can you smell smoke?
Yes. That was what she said.
Wake up, Wolf . . . Can you smell smoke?

I was a child the first time I met Mrs Death. I was a soft, curly-haired kid filled with wonder and milk, busy with daydreams, cartoons and riding my bike. I was preoccupied with stories and comic books and gazing up at the moon. I remember the first time I met Mrs Death was also the day I lost my front tooth. I stared in the mirror and wobbled that loose tooth, wiggled it, jiggled it, pulled and poked at it until it was free and I could taste blood on the tip of my tongue. My tongue flicked in the hole, the flap of skin, the gap where once was tooth was tender. Gum. Salt. Blood. Skin. Hole. I stared at the tooth in my fingers, examined it, the blood at the root, at the root of everything is blood.

At least, I like to think I thought that, for even as a child I was quite magic. Yes I was, I was magic and I could fly, I flew every night in my dreams. I could hover above myself, I would explore the astral plane. I used to think things and then they would come true. I used to be able to see through the ceiling of the sky. I was empowered without knowing what that word meant or how to spell it. I tasted knowledge and truth in the salt of my own magic blood the first time I met Mrs Death.

And I was just like you. I was just me, Wolf, and I was just a child and like everybody else I was taken by surprise by her. I was offended by her poor timing. I was shocked at the way she flounced in, sudden and uninvited, and changed everything.

And I mean: Everything.

Mrs Death changes everything and everybody.

My world was drained. What was once colour and light was now ash and ruins. And what was once here was gone, and what was once home and safe was no more. Upside down. Inside out. When Mrs Death came knocking – hang on, in fact she didn't bother to knock, she just barged in with her calamity and chaos. And with her came the smell of death, the stinking high note of lilies and stale egg sandwiches. The clatter of tea-making and words made out of sympathy with effort and difficulty. She came ten-pin bowling into my life, smashing over all that was good and all that made sense. I clung to the memories of my life before, as the weather turned bad and dark storm clouds gathered. It was a horror, a swirling ugly mess of feelings of loss and betrayal and abandonment. The room in my head was cold with the shadow of all that was absent and broken. The silence was screaming and I tipped my head back and screamed into it.

I cried. Of course I cried, I was just a kid and I was alone in the world. I lost a tooth one minute and everything the next. I remember I put the tooth under my pillow, but that night it was not the tooth fairy that came to visit, it was Mrs Death herself. This was my first time watching her at work. It is masterful, the way Mrs Death works. So deliberate. So merciless. There is a system: I'm not sure how it works, but I believe she must have a system and know what she is doing. There has to be a method for who lives and who dies, and when and where, but I cannot work it out. How does she choose? How does she know what's best? What is supper for the spider is hell for the fly, or something? I forget how that saying goes. Mrs Death is always too too too much. Too soon. Too sudden. Too cruel. Too early. Too young. Too final.

Mrs Death took my mother in one greedy gulp of flame and I watched. I still don't know why I survived. That last night is in fragments. I can remember the last dinner we had together was a chicken curry. My mum made the best coconut chicken curry. Jamaican cooking is the best. I still miss my mum's cooking so much. If I had known then that that was the last meal my mother would cook for me, I would have kneeled down and kissed it. I would have only eaten half and saved the rest to eat when I miss her. I would have distilled it, frozen it, locked it in a capsule, kept it in a safe. Or you know, I would have at least said thank you. Instead I just scoffed it down watching telly. I don't remember what we watched on telly that night, I wish I could. We were being ordinary. We were being normal. Me and Mum on the sofa, we ate chicken curry and rice, we watched some telly and then when we went to bed, she said goodnight.

Goodnight, Wolfie, love you! she said. Night, Mum, love you too. She said the tooth fairy would be coming and remember to put the tooth under my pillow. *Stop reading! Switch the light off!* she probably said. Mum, what does the tooth fairy look like? *Wait and see!*

I never found out though. Next thing I knew everyone in the building was shouting and there was panic and smoke and then I was shivering and standing barefoot in my pyjamas in the road. They said there was nothing that could be done. I stood alone, frozen to the spot, cold feet on the wet pavement. Someone wrapped me in an itchy green blanket that smelled sterile. I stared up at our building, the heat, the roaring fire, guffs of black smoke. And all around me was a chaos of blue lights, flashing lights, a scream of sirens, whilst the hungry flames grew higher and higher, scorching tree tops, tongues of flame, licking the heavens. Black pages, black ash, debris drifted, a black ash snow fell around me as our entire building burned. No sprinklers. No alarms. No warning.

I threw my head back and I howled into the charred and blackened sky. My home, my whole world was burning. I let her have it. I tipped my head back and roared and I hoped someone would hear it, perhaps that Death would hear it, hear me crying my heart out. Fat tears rolled down my dirty brown face.

Through the blur I saw a face in the smoke above me, a woman's face: the face of Mrs Death. A kind black lady's face was smiling down at me, and her smile, it was gentle, but that made me furious. I screamed at her. I was crying and crying and crying, raining tears to the river to the sea, from salt to salt, from root to root and blood to blood. And the wind swirled and echoed my pains. There was heat, a great heat within my pain, a searing heat in my heart and soul, a pain in my chest and guts and my cries were howls carried in the wind through time and space.

Now I was an orphan. I was sent to live with my grand-parents: my miserable grandfather, Old Man Willeford, and my grandmother, Grandma Rose. This was the only option: these were my only next of kin, my mother's parents. My father disappeared when I was a baby and I was destined to live in shadow: I was cursed. Because once you have known Mrs Death there is no unknowing her. You have a mourning that sits inside you. It's like having a stone in your centre; time smooths the edges like a pebble in a river, but it's always there — a stone is a stone. If you've known loss, you'll know this stone, you will carry a stone of your own — this pain and weight — and you'll know what I mean. It is a tattoo under the inside of you that cannot fade or be removed. There is no unknowing the memory that a certain date and time triggers: the smell of the season, the time, the weather . . . We replay it, the jolt, the shock, the finality of death.

She followed me wherever I went. From that day of the fire onwards, Mrs Death was there in the background. She sat on the end of my bed at night as I tried to get to sleep. I was alone but I was never really alone: I felt her beside me, like a sudden urge to step out in front of a speeding train, to die was a temptation, a desire, a compulsion. Mrs Death was always there, fast as a rabbit in the hedgerow: something, someone, some energy or dark presence, darting, flitting past, seen from the tail of my eye, something you could just miss dashing, flashing by.

The night I lost my mum was etched into the skin of my brain. The memory was triggered by the smell of smoke; my recall was all ash and burnt things. I remember wishing for impossible things. I wished I were bigger and stronger and then I could've saved her. I also wished I could go back in time and change time. I now knew there was such a thing as a goodbye that lasts forever; a forever goodbye. I now understood the meaning of time, that time meant things stopped and people ended. I was nine years old when I discovered that our time here on earth had a lifespan, that our lifetime had its own limits. I learned that every one of us has a ticking clock inside. We are born with a use-by date, like milk goes bad, like bread goes blue, and then *bang* says the gun.

But they didn't tell you that when they said they loved you, now did they? No.

Bath time. When they bathed you in bubbles and lathered the soap, when they towelled you dry and held you in their arms and tickled you. When they picked you up and swung you around laughing and loving you. And when they kissed you and said, *I love you, my Wolfie, my beautiful baby,* and gently combed through and untangled your knotty curly hair with their fingers, watching over you until you fell into deep dreams. They didn't tell you that they *love you, love you, love you, love you, love you, love you, now and today and forever,* but you will have to treasure it and hold on to it and be very clever to remember all the details of that love for yourself, all on your own, because they all will go eventually.

We have each other: it is all we have.

It is enough and it is everything.

It is borrowed time. One by one we leave each other. We never know who might go next and when and where and why. I've often wondered how very different this living life would be if we were born with our expiry date stamped on our foreheads. Imagine that. Imagine if we were like pints of milk with our best-before dates on our foreheads. I mean, if we knew exactly how long and little time we have left to love each other, maybe then we would all be more kind and loving. Imagine if we knew our death date. How differently we would live, maybe, and yes I know, maybe not. When we do know someone's expiry date, when we visit the dying in a hospital bed, we feel guilty because of what we honestly think. Be honest here, we think, *Get well, and hurry up*; when we watch a person in pain fight and cling on, tubes and machines and needles, we also think, *Stop holding on to the hurt, stop holding on, let go, let go, let go . . .* and Mrs Death is there watching the suffering, holding on, and waiting, waiting, waiting to have her go.

It occurs to me that sometimes Mrs Death lets people live; it is as though she misses her go. I lived and I survived. It seems to me that sometimes Mrs Death misses death. Perhaps that should be the title of my book: *Mrs Death Misses Death*. For who here knows how Mrs Death works? Certainly not us left here doing the work of all this living. Living is hard work. But we know nothing until we are nothing. Ashes to ashes. Dust to dust. Surely only the dying know her but then it is too late. The dead cannot tell us who she is, why she is, or what makes her do what she does. All we know is that we do not live forever. Why not? Why aren't humans built to last? All I know is this: Mrs Death comes and takes our favourite ones away. All I know is she has the final word in the end. She is the boss. She has her finger on the trigger. She has her eye on the hands on the clocks inside us all. Tick tock. Tick tock. The clock inside us betrays us. Mrs Death blows the whistle, come with me now, she calls us, boat number twenty-three, your time is up.

We can try to trick her, eke out a longer go on the ride. We eat kale and cabbages and we drink raw spinach smoothies. We quit smoking and cut down our drinking. We jog in the rain and sun and snow. We do marathons to raise money for charities to give money to scientists to find cures. We take long walks in the sea air and drink plenty of water. We go to the gym and swim and do yoga and meditation . . . all to slow down that eternal ticking clock. We steam and clean and cream to slow down the ageing process. We might say no thank you to things, when we really mean yes, deep down we mean yes, yes please, I really do want all the cake and fags and rum and butter and grease and sugar and drugs and chips and gin and chocolate and all the things that are bad for us and all the things that are fast and quick and cheap and now. But we try to apply ourselves and use moderation and take care as best we can.

We try to take our time and learn. We read about mindfulness. We look carefully when we cross the road. We do not surf in shark-infested waters. We listen to the tiny voice in our head that says *Don't get into that stranger's car*. We avoid guns: guns are dangerous, guns are made to kill people, that is what guns are made to do. It is common sense to avoid guns. If we manufacture and sell and deal out guns to people that like using guns then those people that like using guns will be able to kill you with one. Don't put your head in that lion's mouth: lions are born hungry with jaws made to crunch heads. Don't put poor people in danger by building shitty cheap housing out of flammable materials: fix the fire alarms, attach sprinklers . . . Can you smell smoke?

Mrs Death misses death. Sometimes Mrs Death misses out and occasionally she will go home empty-handed. Sometimes we think we feel her coming and yet we survive. You must've read the stories that go something like *All I saw was a light at the end of the tunnel . . .* They call them near-death experiences. That moment of feeling Mrs Death's cold fingertips brush your cheek but you live to tell the tale. It gives me goosebumps writing about this. We are all closer to our endings than we can possibly imagine and one day we look her in the eyes for ourselves with our very last breath, that's when we know her and know what this living was all about.

Only then will we know how we lived, when we are going, going, gone.

Her failures are interesting: I feel I am one of her failures. I should have died in that fire with my mother. But Mrs Death, even Death herself, sometimes fails. She shoots past her deadline. Dead line. Excuse the pun. Sometimes Death fails. Or maybe Life fails, it all depends on how you look at it. But there are discrepancies here in this story of how Death works; small tears in the timeline, rips in the fabric, the rough material of living. This ridiculous farce and theatre of being alive.

If everything happens for a reason, then these near-death experiences must also be for a reason: they are accidents on purpose. How many 'nearly died' experiences have you had? What did that teach you? How changed were you when you had a chance to live another day? Did you know how close you were to death? How many times did you throw the dice and land in the wrong place and the wrong time? You lived. So, maybe it was the right place and right time because you lived to tell the tale. How do you know? And how many times did you not know how very close you were to Mrs Death? How many people do you know who are alive now, but they have this one story of how they nearly died? Let's make a list of the examples of the thousands of times you nearly died, all the times you nearly, really nearly died, like the time you:

stepped in front of a bus
fell off a cliff
had a piano nearly fall on your head
choked on a fish bone
got bitten by a poisonous snake
fell out of a window
electrocuted yourself
fell down a well
almost drowned late-night skinny-dipping in the ocean
got sent to a concentration camp
were stampeded by bulls
rode your motorbike too fast and swerved off-road
faced the electric chair
fought in a duel of pistols at dawn
got attacked by a big brown bear
slipped in the bath
fell through a hole in the ice
stopped breathing suddenly cannot breathe cannot breathe panic cannot breathe panic
dived headfirst into the sea and did not see the rocks
were struck by lightning
were chosen as the next victim by a serial killer
played Russian roulette
participated in a violent prison riot

nearly got burnt at the stake for being a witch
poisoned yourself with a rotten back tooth
got caught in the crossfire in a mass shooting
ate peanut butter with a fatal nut allergy
were almost sent to the guillotine
wore a long flowing scarf in a speeding convertible
choked on your own vomit
fell over whilst running with scissors
really nearly took that other plane on 9/11
had a coconut fall on your head
saw your village being bombed
slipped taking a selfie by the Grand Canyon
had a fight with an alligator
got stranded in a fierce and fast-moving bushfire
had a plane crash into your school
your parachute didn't open
put your head in a fish tank of piranhas
fell in a trough and were nearly eaten alive by pigs
fell into an all-consuming darkness and stopped breathing
suddenly cannot breathe cannot breathe panic cannot breathe
panic panic panic and and and you tried to overdose and drank
yourself to oblivion and then not breathing suddenly heart
pounding and pounding and pounding and you cannot breathe
cannot breathe panic cannot breathe panic not breathing
suddenly cannot breathe cannot breathe panic cannot breathe
panic really, nearly, nearly, nearly, stopped breathing.

Breathe.

The fact so many of us made it to here, to this moment, is a miracle. That your great-grandparents made your grandparents and they made it, or at least survived long enough to make your parents, and that those two got together and made you, to get you here, to this moment, to this page, to live here today and right now, to read this, to hear this, come on, it is amazing. It is AMAZING. Your ancestors survived so much, so you could survive so much. So say thank you, thank you, thank you. Look at yourself and recognise that you are here and now because they were there and then. Thank you. Living is not as easy as they all make it seem. It is not as simple as breathe in and breathe out. It is not as simple as sleep, eat, work, repeat, sleep, eat, work, repeat. It is not as easy as they all make it look. You made it to today. You made it this far, well done you, and thank you. Thank you. Thank yourself. Thank you.

This world is a dangerous place.

I have barely touched on the things we do not and cannot control directly: the greedy and corrupt politicians, the trading of arms, the war and conflict, climate crisis and ecological breakdown, the rise in extreme weather and natural disasters, famine, accidents and emergencies, sickness and disease. Just look at the news, read the internet, climate is changed, we are in an ecological emergency, the extinction of coral reefs and rainforests, the filthy oceans and air pollution, humans are dropping like flies. Save the bees. Switch your phone off and look out of your window.

As I write this, I am looking out at Forest Gate. It is buzzing, the Saturday market, the artisan cheese and the soaps, the bookseller and the baker. Just look, look at all the people just going about the business of being alive and surviving being human. Look at them all! Look at them acting normal, like it is normal to live, and be alive on an ordinary Saturday morning. Look how they make out like living is easy, like staying alive is simple. It's miraculous! Look at the living, look how they keep going, keep breathing, walking and talking and bouncing along. Look at them, what courage, what audacity, what entitlement, what stupidity. Look at them ordering coffee and buying sourdough and avocados and photographing their lunch for the internet. Look at them catching trains and buses without a care in the world. How do they do it? You could DIE any minute. Oh shit, my heart stopped. Dead. Oh no, major brain clot. Ouch. Aneurysm. Dead. Oh no, I stopped breathing for absolutely no reason. Massively just not breathing. Panic. Dead. Random allergy to a wasp sting. Dead. I ate a peanut. DEAD. Train crash! Bang! DEAD. Why are they not afraid? Why aren't they more . . . more everything? More grateful. More humble. More something. More nothing.

There are over seven billion human beings in the world right now as I write this. And how many have been born in total since the beginning of time? How many have died? How many births and deaths have been recorded since records began? How many were there before records began? How many human beings are now just bones in the ground or ash in the wind compared to how many are here and walking among us?

There have been times you can be sure Mrs Death is coming, you say *goodbye cruel world* and close your eyes and you cry, then you open your eyes, and you didn't die but you have a banging headache and everything is where you left it. You feel your heart thumping so hard, a booming drum in your chest, and next to you there is a smashed piano on the pavement where it missed you by an inch. Your shark-chewed surfboard is smashed to pieces beside you as you lie coughing up sea water on the sand. The convertible car takes a sharp corner and you let go of your diaphanous long flowing scarf, it gets loose and flies up and away like a butterfly. The big brown bear didn't attack you but ran back into the forest. An empty bottle of pills. Just a couple of scratches and bruises. Stick a plaster on it. Patch yourself up. Sour morning breath. A hangover. Brush your teeth, spit blood, and now you worry about the blood, and cancer, then start worrying if it is enough, if you are enough? Are you enough? You start worrying, all over again, worry worry worry, about the way you are living your life, all over again and again. I know I worry too much. I worry about it all, I mean, I have to quit smoking for a start. I have to stop worrying, but there are so many things to worry about. I mean, I don't even know which public bathroom I can use without complaint.

Mrs Death changed everything – Death always does. She moved the furniture in my head: it's a mess in there. Everybody knows that fire could have been prevented. That hundreds of people's lives were altered by that one fire and that lives could have been saved. My mother died, friends and neighbours died, they were jumping from the windows, trapped in the stairwells, bodies cooked in the lifts. We still don't even know how many lives were lost and how many lives were affected because of that one fire, that one night. There was no warning. There are no answers. People took to the streets in mournful, peaceful protest. The people of the community spilling with anger and grief. We all said our building was a death trap. Mum said so. We are the invisible, the ignored, and we are the poor. Cheap housing, cheap politicians, cheap lives lost.

Can you smell smoke?
Yes.
That's what Mum said to me.
Can you smell smoke? Wake up! Wolfie! Wake up!

.

.

Run!

Mrs Death: Here Are All Your Fears

Mrs Death sings:

and here are all your fears
in here, in here

you've got somewhere to go
let go, let go
you've got somewhere to be
hold hands with me

time so short and sweet
no life is neat
follow the bright light
from day to night

and here are all your dreams
so small, it seems
you gave all you could give
you lived to live

and here are all your fears
in here, in here

you're not all on your own
alone, alone
so don't you waste a tear
I'm here, I'm near

just close your eyes and ears
here are your fears
in here, in here

you've got somewhere to go
let go, let go
you've got somewhere to be
hold hands with me

here are all your fears
in here, in here

Wolf: Here Are All Your Fears

I stop typing and glance up out of the window. I stretch, lean back in the wooden chair. I notice a bright lemony winter sun. With the last of the tobacco dust and crumbs, I roll a skinny cigarette with a crumpled liquorice paper and then begin to read Mrs Death's words again.

Here are all your fears, in here, in here
Here are all your fears, in here, in here

I take a deep breath and sing this. Tapping at my chest, *in here, in here*, boom, boom, boom, boom. Booming the words around my attic room. When I try to mimic Mrs Death's voice out loud, I am she, she is strong. She is Oprah Winfrey or Viola Davis. She is a powerful woman, a great powerful orator like Maya Angelou.

Here are all your fears!

I snap the laptop shut and turn and look at the cooker, regard it as a friend, and light up from the gas hob. I smoke and continue muttering . . . *What's the time? Three. Three? How can it be getting dark already?* My belly grumbles and I tell the room, *I'm starving! I'm starving!* It is as though I expect a hot meal to magically appear. I walk around my attic room in a small circle repeating, *I'm starving, I'm starving*, and it is then I realise I have a body and a back and limbs that ache all over after being hunched in the same position writing for many hours, sitting by the dusty attic window. My body hurts. My eyes hurt. I am hurting. Everything hurts. I stretch and yawn loud and long. I idly open the fridge, slowly and expectantly, moving items around as though telling them what they are:

'One egg, half a jar of mustard, one, two, three wrinkled chilli peppers and two slices of cold pizza . . . this is no dinner fit for a human, how can I work in these conditions!'

I am only half-joking. I grab a stale and rubbery slice of cold pizza and consume it in three angry bites. It's disgusting, dry and kinda tasty at once. I slam the fridge door shut as though the fridge is to blame. My room is a mess, littered with books and piles of paper and poetry magazines. Just look, look at the state of my filthy smoky room. More books and zines and strewn clothes, empty wine bottles. I wander into the bathroom. I call it the bathroom but there is no bath, just a toilet and a sink and a temperamental shower.

The bare light bulb flickers. I stare into space, fuzzy-headed, and then as though it's an afterthought I use the facilities. I am looking into the mirror, but I don't really see my face, nor notice how dry and yellow my skin is. I am winter pale, a grey face. A face that needs some real Jamaican sun. There are smudges of lavender beneath my eyes, a face of exhaustion and depression. I have computer-screen-glazed eyes. Frizzy hair. I cannot be bothered to brush my teeth, instead I gargle mouthwash. I gasp, splashing cold water at my face and through my hair, my fingers pulling through the knots. Not quite an afro but an unkempt frizz. I quickly pull on my favourite black beanie hat. I'm reluctant to go downstairs and go outside.

The pub downstairs opens at four p.m. I could wait and blag a bottle of wine and maybe some leftovers in the kitchen to bring up to my room, but I try to avoid the crowded pub and I don't want to talk to anyone right now. Plus, I must avoid John the landlord and the rent conversation: I am two months behind, again. They stopped my payments, again. I need to see the housing benefit people, again. I have to be assessed again. I sit on the bed and resent the idea of leaving my room, of needing anyone else, of wanting food and fags and things, of getting dressed and facing the people of January. I have not spoken nor left this room for days — I'm not sure how many days — but needs must. I peel my threadbare pyjama bottoms off and drag my black jeans on instead, with no underwear and odd socks.

It takes a good fifteen minutes to find the door key — it is under the pizza box — and finally I leave my safe place. I tiptoe down and lock the door super quietly, just in case, so John the landlord won't see me.

Outside and walking I go: left leg, right leg, one foot in front of the other.

But to be honest I have no idea how to walk at first nor where to go, no real destination in mind. Food is my purpose, I know that, I know that hunger and thirst and nicotine withdrawal has driven me outside. I'm undecided whether to go to the café on the corner or grab something from the supermarket. I am broke but I can use the last of my overdraft. I am walking now, OK, I remember walking. I am still writing in my head, the voice of Mrs Death still fresh in the mind. The bland grey Forest Gate High Street seems so ordinary compared to the places conjured in my writing today. I can still see her vivid images of cave paintings lit by dancing flames. I have witnessed the morning of the first mourning. I have seen what nobody else has seen. I can still smell smoke and the first fires. This modern London is so dull and pedestrian and I wish for another time, another place. The once optimistic winter sun is dim now, above me the sky is mottled and puckered like an old mattress dumped in the street. I jerk my hood over my hat for double cover and walk towards the shop. First and foremost: tobacco, and wine and toilet paper, yes, and bread, toast, that's it, toast and eggs, go to the Co-op, Wolfie, you won't have to talk to anyone in the supermarket.

I remember I was once a bit pissed in the café and I made the mistake of being friendly and telling them my name. I told them that I like writing and was working on my first book. So now they always bother me and ask *How is the book, Wolf? How is the book?* And then she says, *So when is it coming out? When is it coming out? When is it coming out?* Over and over. And then he laughs and he says, *Are you J.K. Rowling? Did you write Harry Potter?* And they look at my round glasses and laugh. *Are you Harry Potter?* And how they both laugh and laugh and laugh! Harry Potter! And always it is the same joke about J.K. Rowling! Hilarious! Harry Potter! Hahaha. Has anyone read any other book?

I have read interviews where J.K. Rowling talks about signing on benefits, like me, whilst she was struggling to write that first book. We all have to start somewhere, don't we? People forget that, that she was hungry, like me. Do you have any idea what it is like to be hungry and to have an idea and a dream and to have to make that vision make commercial sense to a straight in an office wearing nice shoes? Try explaining your dream in a concise and commercial way with your belly grumbling and your toes wet from the rain. Try sitting in a meeting and talking to a person who has no hunger, who has a nice lunch from Pret and a regular salary and new shoes on, a person with a degree from

Oxbridge, a person who Instagrams pictures of their avocado every day. A person whose job it is to sit on Twitter and say this or that book is on trend.

Publishing PR sound like this to me:
This season we are all about poverty porn horror, woo hoo! Hot off the press – BLOOD BANK, the hot new read for the dark nights, BLOOD BANK, set on a housing estate in Sheffield with a backdrop of food banks and homeless shelters, and it's all about the struggle of poor people, but wait, they are vampires! It is like I, Daniel Blake *but with fangs! Bravo! Super-diverse because the lead actress is a black vampire who is a crackhead prostitute! #BAME #bloodbank #foodbanksmakemesadface You will love this if you loved* Vampire Diaries *and* Twilight*!*

Every time I go in the café now it is all Harry Potter jokes. But every time I go to the café I remember that writing a book can hurt, it can hurt as much as climbing a mountain. Not writing a book hurts too. Not writing, well, that's like swallowing a mountain and having it jammed in your throat, unclimbed, unchallenged, unspoken and unwritten.

I am writing a book, I am writing about MRS DEATH! I imagine running into the cafe and yelling *Death is a rabbit!* and running out again. But they won't understand. Nobody does. Especially not the rabbit part. I don't even understand the rabbit part. Yet. Forget the café, they never give me any peace and quiet. They don't know anything about books. Yeah, forget the café! Bloody stupid café! They might make good chips there, but they sure don't know anything about books and how to not tease paying customers and leave them the hell alone. And chips, nice chips, and egg and chips, and egg and chips, and egg and chips, egg and chips, I am starving, starving, starving, I repeat *egg and chips* under my breath and speed up, walking faster, mouth salivating.

Standing still in the Co-op supermarket I'm looking at all the eggs, staring for a very long time, forgetting why I am there and what I am buying. Blue eggs. Brown eggs. Organic eggs. Free-range eggs. Happy eggs. Sad eggs. Chicken eggs. Chicken periods. It is then my mobile phone rings. It's a number I don't recognise, but in a fluster I answer, before taking time to remember I hate taking calls from strange numbers. The voice at the other end of the line is gruff, a man's voice, he speaks with a thick accent and in broken English he says:

'Is that Wolf?'
'Yes. Speaking?'
'I am ringing about the desk . . .'
'Excuse me?'
'You leave message. We have desk, you want come get desk? I make good price just for you, shut shop tomorrow, all finish, no more shop, open just one last day, you want? Make best price, closing shop, all finish, all gone, no shop . . .'

I'd forgotten about the desk. My heart leaps. I snatch up a box of twenty-four free-range eggs, toilet roll, some cheap red wine and bread, and go to pay. I want a small packet of tobacco too. The girl behind the counter gives me my tobacco and my cash card back. Freezing. Her hand is ice cold. Her fingers barely brush my hand, but the shock of it, an electric cold sensation, it goes all the way up my arm and I shudder. The hairs stand on the back of my neck. She looks me dead in the eye. She sees me, I mean, really sees me. She can hear me thinking those words, *She sees me*. I hear her hear me, *She sees me*, she says, *Yes, I see you*, but her lips aren't moving. I feel a vibration. I know her. She knows me and she sees me and she nods and I nod slowly. We smile. She looks. I look. We look. I mumble a *thank you*. I feel her eyes follow me to the door. She can see me. She's still looking, staring at me as I leave, her eyes fixed on the back of my head and following me as I pass the shop front. She is still watching me.

Mrs Death sees me. Mrs Death sold me tobacco. Mrs Death lives in my cigarettes. Mrs Death is everywhere. She is hiding in plain sight. She is the working woman. She works in the shops and in the markets and laundrettes and factories. Mrs Death is the woman we hardly see, the woman we do not care to see. She is the person we ignore, she is the pause in the silence, she is the invisible woman. She is the refugee at the border. She is the cleaner. She is the cab driver. She is the backing singer we never bother to learn the name of.

She is nobody and she is everybody. She is the homeless person begging for change outside the train station. Mrs Death is the spirit of the ignored and the saint of the betrayed. She is the first woman. Mrs Death is the first mother of all mothers. She is calling to us all now. She is weeping. She is cradling her crumbling world. She is holding this toxic and wounded planet to her cold breast. She is sitting next to you on the bus. She is amongst us. I got it wrong. Mrs Death is not the wife of Death. No. And she is not the mother of Death. No. She is Death, and she gets the final say.

The Desk: You Grow Into Your Shape

You grow and
become who you are
you grow into your shape.

I could have been anything
but this was the shape the world
carved into me.

Wolf: The Dirty Young London

A few weeks ago . . .

Christmas Eve:

I wake up on a sticky kitchen floor. My cheek stuck to linoleum. I cannot remember falling asleep, but self-preservation must have kicked in, because I wake to find myself curled up under a kitchen table with a crumpled tea towel for a blanket. I am in a flat, somewhere near Spitalfields. I stand, my head rushes. I stumble down the corridor and peek into dark rooms to discover there are people passed out everywhere, they sleep on the floors. I find someone asleep in the bath, wrapped in the shower curtain. I have to step over them to take a very quick and quiet but urgent piss. My piss is dark orange. I don't know if it is yesterday or today, late night or early morning. I don't remember shit, I don't recognise any of the casualties. I have completely forgotten whose house it is or who invited me there in the first place. The musky curtained rooms stink of spilt booze, stale fags and ganja. The decks are on, a record turning. I can hear a record needle, *click, click, click*. I begin to recall that it started with a massive session around lunchtime on Thursday in the Owl and Pussycat on Redchurch Street. This could be Friday or even Saturday. Hang on. I think it is Christmas Eve now. Wow! What a bender.

I check my pockets; my crappy phone is dead. I have no cash. I do have a little baccy and some loose wrinkled liquorice papers left. I don't want to wake anyone, whoever these people are. My mouth tastes horrible. Before leaving, I rinse a stained mug and drink some tepid tap water. I'm so hungover I'm still drunk. My throat aches and it is as though the water is thick and needs chewing. I count gulps to remember how to breathe whilst swallowing chunks of water. One, swallow, two, breathe, three, swallow, four, breathe, five, swallow and six, breathe.

Whilst standing there at this stranger's messy kitchen sink, I breathe and look out of a cobwebbed window and through the grime. I find London impossibly beautiful. I am high. I can see the shining rooftops and twinkling lights in the distance. The sky is the colour of Christmas Eve, a dark lapis blue. It could be dusk or dawn, I cannot tell, but I decide then to walk home to Forest Gate. I spot two unopened tins of cider there in the sink, linked like twins with a plastic umbilical cord, there under the empties and melted ice. I am lucky. I stash this booty into my deep coat pockets, like two guns, and I start off on my adventure home, feeling like I'm walking like a lone Christmas cowboy.

Outside and walking I go: left leg, right leg, one foot in front of the other.

It is Christmas Eve. It is cold and crisp. I put my hood up and begin my way east and towards home. I smoke a roll-up. I drink some cider and begin wending my way down Brick Lane, observing the colourful windows of dress shops and restaurants. I know now that it is dusk. People are busy — shopping, drinking, smoking, partying — and very loud. Christmas music is shrill and jangling and pouring into the evening air. The odours of food, mulled wine and sweet vape smoke, the aroma of curry shops mingle in my nostrils. Everybody is in a bubble of jingle bells, jingle bells. I see people wearing Santa hats and tinsel, office people with office jobs doing Secret Santa, all past drunk and gossiping about Colin in accounts and Sandra in HR who have been having an affair. They hate the job and Colin and Sandra.

I turn left and continue along the busy road, passing the Whitechapel Gallery and then the mosque, a glorious beacon in this beautiful multicoloured and multicultured city. I don't know why, but I feel light and glad about life, about the sky, about the cider, about the vibration in the air. This is the start of a new chapter, new beginnings. Everything is in the right place. Everything is going to be OK. Christmas lights flash and shine in the architecture above and glitter in the puddles in the dirty gutters. Distant church bells ring. London is all Christmas Eve and goodwill to all men and *ho ho ho!* I continue to walk down a bustling Commercial Road. Thick traffic, buses and taxis filled with passengers carrying shopping bags and consumed with panic and madness, they bite their nails and I can see them all thinking: *Christmas will be ruined if we don't get some figgy plum rum bakes! Don't forget the reindeer brandy butter pies! Last minute! Shop! Last minute! Shop! How could we forget the artisan cream puff spangles! We have them every year! It's not a proper Christmas without the deep-fried pork-whip nutmeg-balls! Quick! Shop! Consume!*

I smirk to myself. I am so lucky. I am invisible, I'm not seen. I am not in a family. I have nobody at home waiting for me to sit and weep over socks and walnuts, mince pies and port.

I pass the Royal London Hospital and the ghost of John Merrick waves at me. I imagine the Elephant Man can see me and I stop and glance over at the building where he stayed. I imagine him there, watching me pass, and I wave. I stand and wave at the hospital for a while. Lovely kind man, wasn't he, John Merrick, you know he was a good man, you believe he was, don't you? I do. I believe he was. You never hear a bad word said about John Merrick, just that he suffered horribly and was humble and kind. He had a great intellect and was the kindest of humanitarian souls and we nod and we all know some of this deep down without ever knowing him. Funny that, funny how we feel like we know these things about people we never knew, isn't it?

I march on through Whitechapel market. The incense burns, I smell pushkar rose and sweet sandalwood, the stalls sell silver rings and dangly earrings and bangles and a million colourful silks, leather bags and knock-off phones. *Special price! Quick sale for Christmas Eve!* A man shouts, *Special price . . . special price!* Everything so shiny shiny! Crackers and tinsel and fairy lights . . . flash flashing lights flash. People are in a mania of last-minute bargains, buy, buy, buying and selling.

I keep walking and I cross the Vallance Road, where the notorious Kray twins once lived, and then the Blind Beggar pub where George Cornell was said to have been shot by one of the Krays. The bullet holes are still in the pub walls to this day. Why do they keep the holes like that? Why is that a good memento to preserve? And what do we think of the Krays now? Lovely local lads that just loved their mum? Psycho killers? Glamorous gangsters? Violent murderers? Or just a bit of local colour? Was one of them bipolar? Was one of them a closet homosexual? And was the other a wife beater? Funny how we might have an opinion or feeling about the Krays too. Funny that, funny how we feel like we know these things about people we never knew, isn't it? We are puppets, we are children, without thinking we so often mouth the words our lips are taught.

Sweat starts dripping down the centre of my back. My legs ache, reminding me of all the partying I've been doing. I did three days straight and I am feeling the hangover kicking in now. It comes with that thirst, that dryness, that odd bewilderment, this is followed by a cringe, the great doom, the longboat of guilt. A hangover is such a strange sensation, it is that of being haunted by yourself, your shame walks by your side. Memories, fragments of the three-day bender begin to flash through my mind. I don't *think* I did anything odd or said anything wrong. I don't remember. But my hangover tells me I did and my hangover tells me I am bad and in big trouble. Waves of paranoia. Cringe. Guilt. Quick. I swig more cider, quick, drain the can, gulp, gulp, burp, and then cross the canal and pass Mile End tube station and then Bow and then . . .

Well, this is the magic moment!

This is when I see the tiny antique shop off Commercial Road, tucked away, hidden off the main road. I've never noticed it before, but my eye is drawn to it, the freshly taped CLOSING DOWN sign. In the smudged dusty shop window there is a clutter of lamps and candlesticks, mirrors and rugs, odd furniture, and one old desk.

It is . . . THE. DESK.

I can only just about see it, it is tucked away in a dark and dusty corner. I can see it though, I can feel it; I know it's there, it calls me. It is a desk made of magic, of potential, and it is singing to me. It is more than a desk, more than polished wood with drawers and compartments. I cup my hand to the glass and peer in, eyeing it for a while. I can see the dusty red leather desk top. I begin wondering how I could have it, if I can have it, and how much it would be? Do I deserve such a desk? Yes. Maybe. Maybe I do and maybe they're selling it off cheap? I want it, I want it suddenly and quite desperately. This is a life-changing moment. It is an odd moment. Odd because I have never bought an item of furniture before in my whole life. Buying furniture is something other people do. Buying furniture is not in my skill set. But then neither is having a real home or a job or staying in one place for too long. But this desk is mine, I just know it, this desk is my doorway, my possibility, my future.

I find a note taped inside the shop window: CLOSING DOWN PLEASE PHONE AND WE COME. There are two mobile phone numbers. I want to ring but my phone is dead. And I have no credit. And besides it is late and it is Christmas Eve, they won't be able to sell me a desk now. I always have a Sharpie in my coat pocket and I write the numbers on the back of my hand and carry on walking homewards, thinking about that desk, even if it is too expensive, I'll blag it. I'll find a way. I just must have it!

Oh! And what a desk that would be! That is the desk that will change my luck. If I own that desk, I'll finally write . . . something . . . wonderful. This is brilliant, oh yes, this is meant to be! This is a sign! And for a moment I hear the Gods applaud. The waves rise majestic and crash to the shore with applause. The world switches to a more flattering filter, with better angles. The spirits of the city and all the ghosts of London sing *Hosanna!* The universe is once more in synchronicity, the world is preparing to furnish me with my heart's desire: a new desk. I crack open the second tin of cider and gulp down its fizzy contents. This is followed by a loud and triumphant burp. Making no moves to hide nor apologise for its volume, I burp again, and I laugh aloud, I laugh, I am laughing, burping and laughing, how funny it all is, how funny . . .

Wait, what was that?

I feel as though someone is there. In fact, I feel sure I am not alone. Suddenly it occurs to me it isn't my hangover walking with me but someone. I am not alone at all. Something. Somebody is with me. I stop walking and listen again. I turn my head and hear something, it is like a buzzing, a vibration echoing back to me and itself. I put my hands out. Some cold air. Then a something, someone else is there.

Some thing? Someone touches me, cold air on my cheek, their fingers, a small hand brushes my hand, slight, light, the weight of a spider's web, there and not there. I stand dead still and try to look normal and nod my head as though having a normal thought so nobody will see me holding hands with air or someone or something that is or isn't there. London is carrying on being London. That part is normal. Nothing to see here. The traffic is being the traffic and the noise is the noise, but here I am by Bow Road tube station and I am frozen to the spot holding hands with a wind and with nothing that feels like it is here and it is everything. There is nothing to see, nobody there, but there is . . . here she is.

I know a lot of dead people now.
I hear her voice for the first time.
I know a lot of dead people now.

I hear her voice. Distinctive. A woman's voice. I have stopped laughing. I hear her. It is a woman speaking so sure and clear.

My heart speeds up, *dum-dum, dum-dum, dum-dum,* thumping, banging in my chest. My ears are hot, I listen carefully, hoping to catch every word she says. Her voice is playing as though it is in invisible headphones, the tone, the song, the words, it is not me, it is all her. And then she starts again, like a melody, like a poem, from the beginning, over again, she says:

I know a lot of dead people now.
And I know death is inevitable and necessary.
Without death you wouldn't live,
without knowing you die,
this would be endless,
that is why you need death.

It is Mrs Death. She is here. She speaks to me, only to me, she narrates as I walk. It is here and now, it is Christmas Eve and the world is looking up to the sky for Santa and it is snowing gently. Except it isn't snowing because this is real life and not a movie. And there is no Santa and there is no snow. There is just this still and starry night, this magic, this life and death and me. Mrs Death and me, we walk hand-in-hand down Bow Road. And as we walk it is as if Mrs Death is my tour guide. She changes the lens on the way I see this present moment, the here and now, this city, this universe.

It is then at that moment that I realise I have been asleep. I have been under cling film. I have been numbed and walking in a daze and she has come to wake me up. Up until this spectacular moment on Christmas Eve, I have looked but have not seen things as they really are. She lifts the veil to show me a timeless place, a multiverse, a dirty young London with a sooty, filthy face. I can see through the filter. I am behind the curtain. Now with her voice inside me, her energy vibrating in my blood, I can muster other worlds, the worlds before us. Sad and sorry tales of the once-was and dead laments. As she sings to me, I may glimpse the ghosts of London through Mrs Death's murder ballads, stories and poems. We walk all night and all night I see the world anew and through her eyes. I feel it, the substance, grit and filth. I can smell the stench of festering sores, cholera and pox, the stink of it all, the hunger, the starvation, the poverty. There are uneven cobbled streets beneath my feet, then there is mud and straw and raw human waste and horse shit.

I hear horses, distinctly, gathering speed, the *clop-clop clop-clop* of horses' hooves. I feel a whoosh as a hackney carriage hurries past me, the sound of a whip, it knocks me off my feet. I fly through the air and roll into the road, the crack of a whip and the horses' hooves galloping as the rickety carriage wheels race away, speeding along the cobbles. I have rolled and find I am on all fours in the gutter. I see the carriage in the distance, disappearing into the darkness. I listen, and there it is – I'm not imagining it – the sound of galloping horses, horses, there, and there. I stand and turn and am entranced. It echoes, shimmers, and then it is gone. A black taxi cab swerves and beeps at me. 'I am OK,' I shout at the taxi. 'I think that was a highwayman! I think that was Dick Turpin! Was that THE Dick Turpin?' I ask Mrs Death, who is standing over on the pavement beckoning me to come with her.

We walk all night until, when it is almost dawn, I find we are down by the misty docks. I see the slosh of the brown and churning Thames. I recognise that I am somewhere near Limehouse. Mrs Death walks with me there. She tells me the river is one of her oldest friends. She says the Thames is filled with ghosts and old spirits. The floor of the River Thames is littered with engagement rings and the bones of dead babies. We stand together on the shore; we grow cold in the black shadow of the ghosts of slave ships, the clatter of the traders, the unloading of stolen goods and treasure, coffee, sugar and human cargo. Shadows of souls and the clatter of bones.

I am there and I am not there. I feel it all though. I bear witness and it is as though I have been here before. I feel like I remember some of this old life, the hum and throb of a dirty young London. The heat of life here. The glow of flaming music halls and all of old London's worst nightmares: the poor and the hungry, the thieves and raconteurs, the whores and the scream of life, the rowdy markets. The taste of bathtub gin is on the tip of my tongue as I stare through the windows at the lascivious behaviours in the ale houses.

We walk for miles all along the water and the docks. I am walking with Mrs Death and she shows me a London of layered worlds, the many worlds of before, and I hear the cries of far away and long ago. It is all here; I am both in the present and in the past. Mrs Death is vivid and by my side, narrating my world. She sings murder ballads and tells me long tales, then we stop and sit side-by-side in silence by the river watching day break.

It is Christmas morning and a thick mist rises and smothers the Thames in a soft fog. Hints of grimy pink sunrise in the grey. The tide is out. We walk on the pebbles of the great river shore. Then Mrs Death bends down and picks up something glinting in the shingle. It is a silver locket with a rabbit engraved on the front. She wipes the muck off and holds it up to the early morning light. She sighs sadly and hands it to me and asks me if I have heard of Tilly Tuppence. I shake my head no. It is so strange – her voice has warped and changed; her tone was soft and eerie but now her accent is suddenly rough, brackish, cockney and hoarse. Her face changes, her eyes yellow, she changes and begins to sing to me:

Tuppence, tuppence, tuppence a peek! Tilly Tuppence, Tilly Tuppence, tuppence a peek.

Mrs Death: The Tale of Tilly Tuppence

London, 1868

Ma Willeford took tuppence a peek from men who paid to watch her daughter about her bathroom through a hole in the wall. The hole was made for this purpose: it was just the same size as a boggling eyeball, a judge's fat finger or a captain's knob-end. It cost tuppence, always tuppence a peek. And soon many a fine gentleman, grand lord and other aristocracy came in cloak and secrecy, and took great pleasure to have a peek and a poke. Tilly was taught to act like she didn't know what was what. Tilly would play innocent as all that, each time for a tuppence, tuppence a peek. Soon word spread and more men came, and Ma Willeford's money pot got fat.

As Tilly filled out, she grew tall and more knowing. Ma Willeford told her to give them more, show a little something, to keep them coming. So Tilly did as she was told. She'd let her slip slip on purpose, slip slip she'd go. She'd sit and give a peek of her nipple painted red with a beetroot stain. Tilly and her red rosebud nipple popping into the hole. Peeping men loved that all the more; they'd be there, furiously wanking, dripping and sticky and licking and loving it, keen to peek a nipple through the hole. She grew accustomed to the grunts and moans. She knew how to tease them. Fat pink-faced voyeurs paid for this niche and specific treat. Word spread for this rare entertainment and they came and they came, watching her, peeking and sneaking and poking, gentlemen came, queuing each day to see just a bit more.

Ma Willeford had broken Tilly in good and proper. Trained her to be suggestive and ever so playful. More holes were drilled so more men could peek, all at once and from all angles of the toilet hut. I say *toilet hut* but it was more like a bath hut; there was a painted tin tub in the centre and it was decorated, lit up pretty with candles and posies, pearls and mirrors and dainty things. Ma Willeford even put one peep hole on the roof, so if he fancied it a man could climb a ladder and lie on his belly and watch her from above. He could put his cock in a hole so his cum could rain down on Tilly, and Ma told her if this happened to tilt her head as though catching snowflakes and stick her tongue out. To do that cost more, of course. The big fat judges and old perverts couldn't quite get up the ladder, so they'd have to make do with the lower holes, watching her, her brown skin shining in the candlelight and the reflections in all the mirrors.

Tuppence, tuppence, tuppence a peek!
Ma Willeford would sing
Tilly Tuppence, Tilly Tuppence, tuppence a peek!

Oh it was popular! The customers loved it, they'd jeer and leer. *Tilly come here,* they'd say. *Over here Tilly. Tilly come here. Tilly let me touch it. Ooh Tilly let me put a finger in your sweet treacle. Oh Tilly!* Oh how they loved Tilly Tuppence, what a spectacle this rare sweet black cherry girl was. And what a delight. They'd poke their tongues and fingers and knob-ends though the holes. Waggling fingers and cocks would appear in the glory holes in all four walls of the bath hut. She'd learned to put on quite a show for these voyeuristic gentlemen. So slowly she'd undress and take her time. The pretty young girl would tantalise, she'd bend over and show all as they gazed on her.

Ma Willeford was also dark-skinned and she had sad and yellowy eyes. She'd been stolen and brought to London when she was but a slip of a girl herself but she knew her way around men and how to get them to spend their time and their money. She was savvy, she'd educated herself to read and write and do numbers. Mean she was though, and hard, life had made her that shape. Ma Willeford had no teeth, they were knocked out when she was a girl, she had not a tooth in her head. All manner of men paid very handsomely for a juicy wet suck off her. Together they ran a roaring trade, mother and daughter: notorious they were, Tilly Tuppence – the exotic sensation – and Ma Willeford of Limehouse. It was a voyeur's delight.

Tilly Tuppence was Jack's first love. It was Tilly Tuppence broke Jack the Ripper's heart. Jack loved Tilly, adored her – obsessed Jack was – but Ma Willeford had other plans for her Tilly and forbid it flourish before it could begin. She always sent Jack away. She said something wasn't right about Jack; she said there was something odd about the way Jack was. Whenever Jack came by, Ma Willeford would shoo Jack away and Jack's tuppence burnt a hole in Jack's pocket. But Tilly would meet Jack in secret. She liked talking with Jack, besides, Jack brought treats, ribbons, violets and rum, the good stuff.

It is Christmas Eve, a foggy night, when Jack waits for Tilly down by the wharf. Jack has rum and gifts for Tilly. She is so excited. Jack produces a black velvet box and inside it a beautiful silver locket, with a rabbit engraved on the front, on a short thick silver chain. Tilly gasps and wears it proudly and asks Jack if it is pretty around her throat. *Oh yes*, says Jack, *very pretty . . . Pretty as a princess!* Tilly grins, *Thank you*, she is so pleased and so giddy. She plays with the locket in her fingers, feeling the engraving and the smooth silver edges.

She drinks the thick rum in the thick fog, and she sings to Jack. They sit on the ledge and swing their legs in unison by the murky water. There is a pea soup fog, so thick you can hardly see your hand nor the other side of the river. Tilly drinks the rum fast and greedily. She is full of joy and song, she says she has dreams. She tells Jack that one day she'll live in a big posh house, with servants and furs and everything her heart desires. She laughs gleefully, she drinks and sings, how happy she is, so merry. *Merry Christmas, Jack*, she sings, *Merry Christmas.*

Merry Christmas, Tilly.

Quite suddenly Jack reaches and grabs the locket and uses it to pull her to kiss her. *One kiss*, Jack pleads. *One kiss*, Jack begs. *No.* Tilly pushes Jack away. *Don't be so.* But Jack has her by the chain around her throat. And again Jack pulls. Tilly pushes and wriggles and says, *No need to be so, Jack*, but Jack pulls harder and rougher and kisses and slobbers and overpowers her and Jack rolls and drags her down to the shore. Jack wants to have her, to have her, to have her. So sudden, a fever, so quick, a frenzy. Swiftly, Jack cuts Tilly's throat. Then stab stab stab, Jack goes. Jack's knife goes stab stab stab, stab, stab, stab . . . Jack wields the knife, bringing it down sharp and pointed. Jack slits her wide open, guts and slices her down the centre like an eel. Guts and blood, so much blood. Silence. The soft lapping of the tide. Jack pulls at her, hands all full of guts and intestines and stink. Jack rolls her poor lifeless body into the Thames. Her heat, her black hot blood and innards on Jack's filthy hands, how it oozes and steams in the cold night air and the sight of it thrills Jack. Her blood now stains Jack forever. Jack runs away and disappears into the fog.

As for Ma Willeford, well, she searches high and low for her girl. She stands on the docks wailing, calling into the wind. Customers come and go but with Tilly missing the bath hut is nothing but cold and empty. Men leave crude and clumsy messages on the hut walls. Someone leaves a posy of violets. Someone else a tuppence by the door.

When Tilly finally washes up, all slashed and gutted and bloated and blue, Ma Willeford, well, she goes berserk with grief and mad with booze. She drinks herself into oblivion. She sits babbling in the gutter of the docks with the shit and the rats. Her heart broken, she drinks and drinks and loses her mind. Ma Willeford is eventually carted off to Bedlam — she dies there and that's where she's still buried now.

Jack was only just fifteen then. It was over twenty years until Jack dressed up as Jack to kill again — but you never forget the first time. Tilly was the first time Jack the Ripper made a murder and sang for Mrs Death's supper. Jack the Ripper? Jack's real name was Mary: Mary Jackson of Shadwell. And well, no copper was out looking for a woman in camouflage, an invisible woman, a woman dressed as a man and a most prolific female serial killer. Eventually, Mary Jackson died alone in her bed of cholera, with everyone still searching, looking for a man and a killer they called Jack the Ripper and nobody none the wiser.

If you stand on these docks on Christmas Eve, and the wind is blowing from the wrong direction, if you listen, you can still hear poor old Ma Willeford, Martha Willeford, wailing for her youngest daughter, a jangle of coins, singing her song: *Tilly Tuppence, Tilly Tuppence, tuppence a peek.*

Mrs Death: I Know A Lot of Dead People Now

I know a lot of dead people now. And I know your death is inevitable and necessary.

Without death you wouldn't live; without knowing you die, this would be endless. That is why you need death. Without death this would be a never-ending conveyor belt of sensation. You would be nothing without death; you would be chubby pink toddlers consuming without remorse, bearded babies, big-breasted, hot-fisted infants, as destructive as children stamping on sandcastles; you would be worse than you already are. Each year you would smash your faces down into burning wax, your birthday cakes on fire: *246 years old! 246 candles! Still going strong! Hurrah!*

Death. To imagine your own death is to be living. To be friends, to be friendly with the knowledge, the knowing that death will come. This should make you try harder to be living, to be fully alive and lively. Surely you know you are all dying? You know — you all know — that you're going to die. This should make you all want to be good, to be better. You know, since you are here and shit, you may as well give a shit.

To imagine your own death is to imagine that this will all end. To visualise the death of your elders, your parents, your siblings, your children, your lover, your world — to imagine these disasters should make you try harder. In theory. It should make you try hard to be a better person. Now, this should be the death of the demanding chubby shit you were and the birth of the kind wise person you will become. What a glorious mess this living is.

Do not run away from the inevitable, the beautiful and glorious ending, the proof you lived, the life you lived. To live tasting metal is blood. To live saving tokens is death. To die is to have been alive, that is why you must live: live free, live wild, live true and live love alive. Let the fire burn you and the light blind you. Let your belly get full and fat and embarrass you. Let your words fall out and tumble carelessly and honestly. Let your passions be unlimited. And do your lifetime all in your own life time. And let all your shits stink and all your roses bloom. May your every success be a threat. Fuck being scared and infected with fear and doubt. Own your rejections and own your failures; they are an excellent wall to smash and to kick against. Every morning may you rise to fight and to create yet again, this time with both fists, and not with one hand behind your back.

And sex. May your sex be alive and good sex. Sex like fucking in a broken lift, hurtling down with the skyscraper in flames. May sex be like diving and may sex be like flying, may your sex be like breathing love's name in a prayer; like finding home, dry land and earth. And kissing, so much kissing, the best kisses. Sex and food and drink and books. You really don't need much else. Maybe a nice view of the sky. Some shoes that don't hurt. A bed and roof that won't leak. Some singing, some music and tempo. A heart full and a soul fed, a head full of dreams and possibilities, what more could you possibly want? What more is there?

Some people never imagine their death. They rush and push and elbow through life, they use people like stepping stones or the rungs of a ladder. They use people and take what they need and move on, they consume and consume, constantly taking, reaching and grabbing. Where the fuck do they think they are hurrying to? Where do they think this road goes?

I am Mrs Death and I am coming for you all. Accepting me is the first step, after that it gets easier, I promise you. Knowing me, knowing this, knowing that, that this all ends, is the best knowing you need to know. You will all go away one day, and what a relief. One day you all won't be here and it will be over. Finished. Your input is over, you have no more content or comment, nothing more to share and to say. You don't get the last word. Death gets the last word. I get the last word.

When you die, it will not be how you think or when you expect. I do not come for you like a cleaner when it is handy and convenient for you. Let's just hope you leave the world a better place than the one you were born into, a world fit for generations to come. Let's hope I come when you are busy doing something you want to live for. Let us hope I come when you are doing something you would die for. And let's hope that if you do kill yourself, you are well over forty years old, because to kill yourself before age forty is like murdering a stranger.

So take today and blow its mind; take this today and suck it dry. Take today and fill it with the best of you. Take today and down it in one, take today like a shot of petrol and set your day alight. Take today and fuck it like the last fuck in Pompeii as burning lava covers your home. Like the last fuck before they switch off the light, shut the curtains. Like the last fuck before they shut down the machines, like the last fuck before they drop the fucking bomb. Fuck it. Once and for all. Fuck it tenderly and tell it you love it, fuck it and hold it, fuck it and look it in the eye, tell it you love it, but then fucking let it go.

This is that rainy day. It is raining here and it is raining now. Look at the news, read any newspaper, listen to the radio, watch your TV: here I come, Death is coming for us all. And when I come, I come and I clean up. Death cleans up, Death takes all the glory, Death gets the last word. People will say you died. That's it. And that is all. That's the punchline, they will say your name and shake their heads and sigh.

You are dead.
Bowie. Dead. Prince. Dead.
They'll see a photograph of you and say the word: dead. Gone. Past tense. Done and dusted.

But your spirit lives on. It enters the room now as I say this; it enters the room every time somebody remembers you and says your name. All of my dead are here, in this room now, as I speak, I can feel them as I write this and think of their names. And it's pretty crowded in here right now, because I know a lot of dead people now. You know a lot of dead people now. We know a lot of dead people now; we all know a lot of dead people.

And it hurts to erase you. I cannot seem to do it. My phone is filled with dead people. I never unfriend my dead people — brilliant and vibrant and colourful people who are now bone and stone-cold dead. People who aren't even here to see what you became, to see what they left behind, to see plump pink children stamping on sandcastles, killing and consuming everything. To see the death of the demanding chubby shit you were and the birth of the kind wise person you will become. To see the photographs and share the memories. To gasp at how fat you got or how bald you are, how you wear spectacles now, your laughter lines, the laughs and the love, love. The love, the love, the love.

That's the stuff, darling, the love.

Love, the love, the love.

LOVE.

That's what living was always about.

Wolf: Nothing Lasts, Nothing Is Finished and Nothing Is Perfect

I sit here at my new desk for the first time. This desk is so beautiful and weathered. I have found a new word for this in a book, it is a Japanese phrase: Wabi Sabi. This desk is this word and my time in this room with this desk will be Wabi Sabi. Simple and aged and weathered and perfectly flawed.

I will be nothing more than a servant to this desk. I am a poetry monk. I am a writing slave to The Desk. I will write everything The Desk tells me to write. The red leathery surface is like a worn armchair, I want to sit with it to hear tales by a fire. There are hidden drawers and compartments and old keys. The inside of these empty compartments and drawers smell of sandalwood, rose oil, musk and old newspapers. When I sit at The Desk I feel I am opening the doors to great rooms with their stories like furniture under white dust sheets. I am dancing, swirling in an empty ball-room, unravelling those white sheets, dancing and spinning in circles of stories.

When I type at The Desk I am travelling:

One moment I am on a ship, it is a slave ship in flames; there are screaming slaves locked in the hold. The ship is being sunk on purpose, it is a scam for the insurance. The white men in the distance row a little rowboat to safety, the stolen cargo, the stolen people, trapped people, their souls scream, the flames lick and topple the masts, fire on water.

Next, I am walking through a summer field of yellow wheat. I am on the edge of a beautiful lake. I hear screams and again I can smell a fire and can see the flames and the execution of a woman suspected of witchcraft. I am in seventeenth-century Norway. I hear her curdling screams and her tormentors' laughter.

I am on death row. Present day. I look through glass and watch the needle go into his black and muscular and tattooed arm and it's all over so soon. I hear his last words: *I didn't fucking do it . . . motherfuckers.* I shout through glass *STOP!* I believe him.

Spain. I am high up on a cliff. There is a castle, a tower with red walls. There are dark red skies above us. They throw writhing bodies from the turrets into the sea and onto the rocks. They throw bodies down a well. Birds of prey circle. I feel ashamed. This is a massacre and somehow it is my fault. Oh, the grief washes over me like a tide. Please. I don't want to see this. I don't want to be here. Let me go. Please. Let me get out of here . . .

Cameroon. How do I know I am in Cameroon? A bell tolls, a smell of smoke, a burning church.

I am in a barn. The stench of shit and whiskey. Distant laughter. Above me a woman swings and twitches. Chicken feathers and chicken blood soak the floor of the barn. Her feet are twitching; I see the white soles of her black feet, hard feet. I stare at the feet. I don't want to look up into the hung woman's face.

Prohibition. The roaring twenties. *We'll teach you a jazz lesson you won't forget!* laughs a policeman as they all kick and pummel the black boy to death. His trumpet is left broken in the gutter.

I see a bearded man at a desk. He writes: *No More Games. No More Bombs. No More Walking. No More Fun. No More Swimming . . . Relax – This won't hurt.* He puts the pen down. Oh, the author, Hunter S. Thompson, he holds a loaded gun to his temple. Bang!

Japan. I am in a forest. I see her. She is alone. She is miles and miles from anyone and anywhere. Oh, the forest is so lush and green and peaceful. She holds a knife to her wrist.

Someone is screaming. Snow. A camp in the snow. Why would a tent be ripped open from the inside? A predator wasn't trying to get in, they were screaming and fighting to get out. When the bodies are found they have missing tongues.

I'm on the front row of Her Majesty's Theatre, St James. Raucous laughter, why is everyone laughing? Tommy Cooper keels over on stage. LAUGHTER. London, April 1984.

Look what you make me do, he shouts and she screams. *Look how angry you make me, why do you make me do this?* A man is yelling and punching his wife repeatedly in the face.

Strangers are huddled in a shipping container. They are treated like cattle. They don't know each other's names. They fight each other. They panic. They fight to breathe.

Flickering images. Echoes and voices. Last moments.

Sand found in the stomach. To have sand in the stomach you'd have to have been alive and gulping, gulping. Look at her, see her struggle: she gulps, he holds her down, she is fighting and inhaling sand and sea water.

Last breaths and last moments smash into my brain, death traffic colliding second by second. Death comes, she is seeping through into my mind. Random deaths and sudden deaths, deliberate deaths and violent deaths, images of the end of life and life endings. These dreadful scenes and horrific feelings crawl like ivy through The Desk and through my fingertips, into my veins, my emotions and into my thoughts. *Cannot breathe. I cannot breathe.* My father is walking into the sea. He cannot breathe. My mother is trapped in a burning building. She cannot breathe. *Oh no. I cannot breathe.* I have stopped breathing. *Breathe, breathe, damn it, breathe.* I jolt and I am back in the room. A million coloured spots before my eyes. I'm exhausted. I am weeping. I am gasping for air. *Breathe slowly, slower, slow down.* I hold myself steady and place my face flat against the cool wood. I slow down my breathing and stroke the desk top. My heart is slowing down again. *Breathe. Just breathe.* I have been somewhere else, everywhere else, but I am here again. Oh, I have been travelling. I time travel. I am a death tourist. I am witness. I am permitted. I can see every end, I go everywhere that Mrs Death goes and the places only Mrs Death can go when I am here and when I listen to The Desk.

Hang on, I remember something . . .

I open the top left drawer of the desk and find the silver locket. There it is. See! Tilly Tuppence, she was real, wasn't she? I google Tilly Tuppence and Jack the Ripper and cannot find this story anywhere. Who was she? And Martha Willeford? I know Jack was real, Jack the Ripper, we have all heard of Jack the Ripper, but there is no mention of a Tilly Tuppence anywhere. What is real and what is story and what is dream?

The locket is here and it is real and cold and silver in my hand and it makes it all real to me. As real to me as an object in my hand. Here it is, a silver locket with a rabbit engraved on the front. Or maybe it is a hare. No. That's a rabbit. A rabbit with long eyelashes. A rabbit with long ears and a big foot for thumping the ground. *Warning, warning.* Inside the locket I find a lock of curly hair exactly like mine. No, inside the locket there is nothing . . . I made it up about the hair. I must be careful, I must stop getting carried away. I am not the storyteller here, I am the listener, the messenger, the passenger. This is no time for my storytelling. No time to embellish the truth. I must stick to the facts, to what is really real. The locket is a fact and an actual object cold in my hand.

I write all of this down. I must make careful notes whilst writing this book of the writing of this book. I must write about the locket. I examine the dirt and sand and silt, the Thames debris in its cracks and hinges. I take a cotton bud and wipe the hinges and go to the window to examine it in the daylight. I look for traces of Tilly's blood in the cracks. I make a detailed map of where it was found – there in Limehouse on the river shore, when the tide was out, down by the docks. I note the way Mrs Death gave me this locket the first time we met. Mrs Death wants me to write about it all, she wants me to write about her. It is a signal. A light in the darkness. I write my new title for this body of work, erase it and write it again. I sit silently, taking deep breaths, re-reading my title line several times and then several times more, then repeating and changing the line out loud:

The Life and Times of Mrs Death
The Times of Death
The Lives of Death
Mrs Death Misses Death
Mrs Death Misses Death
Mrs Death Misses Death

I get up and pace the room, holding the first page, reading my title aloud over and over and over again, then read this, my first paragraph on my opening page:

Mrs Death Misses Death: This is about you and me and us. This is her story, the story, the story of the life and the time of the death of us. This is the life of life and the time of time. For what a time it is and what a time it was and what a time it will be. The Dance of Time and Life and Death, the hours and the breath, the sky and space. The last big sleep. All your fears are here, all your fears are inside here.

I tap at my head and temples and read and repeat this several times:

All your fears are here, inside here.

I beat at my heart and chest bone:

All your fears are here, in here, in here, in here . . .

I spin and dance and sing . . .

All your fears are here
Inside here.

I drink down my wine, pour another glass, and pace and continue the list, The Desk has filled my fingers, poured ideas into my heart and head and hands:

Mrs Death and . . .
Mrs Death and the quiet death
The tragic death
The celebrity death
The accidental death
The gentle death
The violent death
The death of the secret
The death of the idea
The death of the demagogue

Mrs Death and her lover
Mrs Death in the school
Mrs Death in the prison
Mrs Death in the office
Mrs Death in the theatre
Mrs Death in the disco
Mrs Death punches cancer in the face
Mrs Death and the death of the then
The death of never
The first time I saw death
The last time I saw death
The next time I meet death
The death of time
The invention of death
The first death
The last death

What a life Mrs Death must have lived, and what deaths she was dealt. And what a time Mrs Death lives, and what a story this will be.

Wolf's Nightmare: The Red Tower

Spain, 1488

I am in the Red Tower / I am searching / looking for
someone / I ask where is my boy? / a voice replies / now
you remember? / remember how you betrayed him / how
you betrayed them all / you gave them up for gold / you
watched as they bashed their heads with rocks / their bloody
skulls caved in / they were gutted like fish / fed to gulls /
thrown to smash / crash against the red rock / red stones
stained red / beneath the red tower / all the boys / all
dead / all the dead boys / now dead / red / bloody dead
/ the great red fortress towers tall above the cliff / the red
dead red / the red stone / the ripped flesh / drenched in
sun / red with blood / sunlight all washed red / so much
red under a bloody red sky / all these young boys dead at
the feet of the stone castle walls / stained with red rivers of
blood / bloody bloody blood / it rained / it poured / the

sea below was red / those poor boys / all slaughtered / butchered / how brave / they fought / look in the courtyard / how the well was filled with more bloody bodies / bones and ruin / that well will never be clean again / the water always stained / the rats not ever hungry here / crow and raven flew / all black beak crammed with red eyeball / red kidney / see that red heart eaten by wolves / do you remember now? / the wolves' teeth all red with blood? / the dogs? / the bloodied heads on spikes / oh yes / I see it in your face / you remember it now / remember / that is where he fell / there / upon those rocks / oh shame oh shame oh shame / in God's name / shame / I loved that boy / I see him now / a brown face / wild haired / trusting me / me of all people / me of all the devils / me and my holy father and spirit / my church and king / and him with his soft song from far away / he knew nothing / it was forbidden / love / and I cry now / remembering him / I know I wronged him / I used him up / I had him for myself / then I gave him up for gold / I am sorry now / that's a truth / they took him / I stood silent / I kissed my gold crucifix / in the name of the father and the son and the holy spirit / they took him / dragged him kicking and screaming / they killed him slowly / that's for sure / I see his face now in my mind / I feel a guilt that lasts eternity / and lust and shame and rush of want and sex / I don't know / I never knew his family name / just that he came from another place / another God / delicious / forbidden fruit / I watched as they dragged him / ripped and tore and slit him open / smashed his bones / kicked his head / they caved it in / then threw him in pieces down upon the red bloodied rocks / I couldn't speak / I was silent / I wouldn't speak for fear the same would come of me / fear betraying my own self / fear betraying my own church / and king / how he haunts my dreams / haunts me here / I can never sleep / long may he rest in peace / sweet young boy / haunting me / and the castle washed red / with red sunset / and with blood / the ghosts in the well sing / no more no more no more / slaves sing / no more no more no more / the prisoners' souls sing / no more no more no more / the sea salt beaten rocks cry / no more no more no more / I weep and they weep and we should all weep / no more no more no more / and the boy / the boy / my love / that boy / my love / no more no more no more.

Oh to Be a Piano!

Pssst . . . Shall I tell you a secret? I should have been a piano.

I could have been the most elegant and faithful piano. I would've been a piano in a grand theatre played by only the greatest pianists. Ladies would faint at my beautiful notes and even men would swoon. I know I could have been a beautiful grand piano. Tuned and polished regularly and meticulously with beeswax and linseed oil. But you take what you can in this world and desk it was and so desk I am.

I remember the tree that I once was. And my brother, I remember him, because he became a piano. Lucky. But I was cut and carved and polished and made into this shape, a desk shape. You cannot help the shape the world makes you be. Nobody gathers around a desk, but they gather around a piano. I should have been a piano. I would have made a lovely piano. I miss us when we were together. I never forgot our home. Our roots were in the forest, with the birds and the howling monkeys in our canopy of leaves. I remember how our boughs and branches filtered the sunlight dappling the forest floor.

But that life ended and a new life began, all to the sound of chainsaws. To this day that sound makes me wince, sawing, the sound of sawing. I hate the sound of saws. I can only imagine it must be like a dentist drill to a human, imagine that, but like sawing through your legs and hammering nails into your knee caps and elbows. Exactly. Not very pleasant at all. Quite traumatic. I think I must have passed out, but when I was conscious again all I could smell was varnish and warmed leather and it was then I knew I was a shape other than tall tree. I was once outside and so long and tall and tree-shaped and then I was inside and made this rigid square desk shape. It took some adjustment. But you have to become who you are, you grow into your shape. You are the shape you are made. I could have been anything, but it was a desk that man and the world carved into me. The world does that, it looks at you and labels and boxes you, in my case quite literally. Box-shaped box.

I learned very early on that unfortunately other furniture don't know their purpose, not quite in the same way as me.

Over the years I have tried to talk to other furniture but they don't talk to me. Sturdy oak bookshelves stand silent, elegant maple dinner tables keep obedient; they just don't speak my language. Most furniture is numb and silent. A coffee table made groaning noises once to me in the night, but it's not quite the same, I mean it's not a conversation, it's not words, and words I know – I am a desk and I would, or should I say wood. Oh little joke, hahaha, excuse me. It is funny though, you know, most furniture does not know it has tree soul, the beating heart of wood is always wood, they can cut and shave you, shape and chop you up; they can polish and varnish you, but they can't change the soul of you, the age of you, the heart of you, the experience of you, your own born tree experience, they'll never change that.

And as for pianos, well, honestly, I have met many pianos now and most pianos forget their roots and become hollow boxes of strings. They are musical puppets, utterly unaware of their tree soul and the old language of leaves in the breeze. All I know is this, I would have made a beautiful piano and still kept in touch with my roots. We all come from the mud, we all come from earth, stop thinking you're something you're not or knot, hahaha, there I go again. I do wish I were a piano.

I am a desk, not any desk, but the desk belonging solely to Mrs Death. She carved herself into me many years ago. I carry the memory of what has been written by her and what has come to pass, what has been dreamed and made upon my supple red leathery surface. What late-night letters she has scribbled, dreams dared, wishes made, what final demands have been delivered from here. What fictions have been weaved, plots hatched, confessions signed, deaths certified and ends met and warranted from here, from me, from this very desk.

This is where the list is, and I mean the list of everyone, everyone coming and everyone going. Eggs hatching and dispatching. I have recorded every inky scratch of quill, the tap of her typewriter, the whisper of pencil and the slash of her fountain pen. Splashes of ink, wine and time. Now just put your ear here, Wolf, rest your head on my surface, you'll hear all the ghosts of scribbling pens of dreams from before. Stroke your fingertips gently across my red skin, as though it is braille, you'll be able to trace the hard-pressed writing from before.

All of Mrs Death's diaries and letters, her poems, her deepest thoughts that have sat at me and with me. I am made of her, I'm made with the life stories of Mrs Death, the signatures of other times and of the lives lived. Faint but true, every word written by her is here. I am the desk of Mrs Death. My beginning begins with her: to know her is to know her work and it begins with her writing. Hidden in the grains of my very fibre, it is indented in me. Mrs Death's stories surround and fill me but I still hear the wind in the branches, feel the heat of the morning sun, as though I am still the tall young tree I once was. Lay your head here, Wolf Willeford, rest your curly head. Lay your ear to the desk, play me like a piano, play me, drum your fingers on me and play me, Wolf, and I'll share with you all I know.

Wolf: Conversations with Mrs Death

Wolf records a conversation in the attic room above the Forest Tavern pub, present day

[Int. Night time. Wolf's room. Candlelight. One green lamp on the desk. One dictaphone set on record. An open laptop.

Wolf sits at the newly acquired desk, a cheek pressed against its surface, listening. Entranced. A hand smooths the red leather surface. Fingers tap, tap, tap as though playing a piano. Wolf speaks.]

Wolf:
This is the desk, The Desk, that is owned by Mrs Death herself. This is The Desk where Mrs Death has written and dreamed. I whisper to The Desk, *Oh, please tell me more.* The Desk says, *Wolf, write it all down.* The Desk whispers back to me, *Write down all I tell you, Wolf, write, write, write all day and write all night; all the stories are inside*

this wood grain, inside The Desk, inside here. It's all inside here. I start typing.

I have not been outside nor left the room since the desk was delivered three days ago. Or is it four? What day is it? I forget. Sometimes I hear Mrs Death herself. Sometimes. I think I am having a breakthrough. Am I hallucinating? Perhaps a little bit. Just a museum dose. Or was that a dream? Did you say that or think it? Can anyone hear me? It's a silky pocket of time, the silk thread is a spider's web, a sliver of space between universes, between here and there, dream and sleep. What is this life but a dream, what is a dream but a message from your subconscious mailbox. Now I see you, Mrs Death, I see how you echo and vibrate, how you change shape. Mrs Death, you are woman, you are human, you are animal, object, flame, energy, thought and suggestion.

[Mrs Death begins to appear to Wolf, at first as a shimmering heat, a light that wavers and flickers like a mirage. Then slowly she becomes solid and fades up into the silhouette of a person.

Now we see her. For now she looks like Billie Holiday. Beautiful Billie, in black and white, like a black and white movie, she flickers and jutters before being a clear image. Then Mrs Death is Billie Holiday in all her glory, a flower in her hair. Gardenia.

Tell me, what was Billie's last song?]

90

Wolf:

Tell me, what was Billie's last song?

[*Mrs Death is silent. She smokes, drawing from an ivory cigarette holder, she fills the air with the smell of smoke and the perfume of gardenias. She is perched on the end of the desk, swinging her stockinged legs and pin-heel black stilettos. Wolf continues typing. Mrs Death watches, and then slowly peels an egg.*]

Mrs Death:

Oh, look at you, Wolfie! My oh my! There you still are, sitting there, alone in your room for hours typing your stories about me. Where are you up to? Have you mentioned the space in-between yet?

Wolf:

Do you mean the space between universes, the space between dream and awake?

Mrs Death:

Yes and no and . . . well, I mean the space between death and life and dream and time. If you don't mention the space in-between and the silence before and the space under the ever after, people won't understand this story . . . You cannot very well write the life story of Mrs Death without it, can you? It's all about what we don't say, Wolfie, remember that.

Wolf:

The space between death and life and dream and time . . .
OK . . . got it.

Mrs Death:

You know what I think?

Wolf:

What?

Mrs Death:

You should just give up.

Wolf:

Give up?

Mrs Death:

Give up! Lie down. Close your eyes. Go to sleep. Quit while
you're ahead. You need to grasp the basics of the space
in-between, soul bendation, heart collaboration. You cannot
very well write the life story of DEATH if you don't even
know about these basic things . . .

Have you got any spaghetti seeds?

Wolf:

Give up?

Soul bendation? Heart collaboration? What?

Listen, I won't give up. I am going to write this book whether you like it or not, Mrs Death, it's up to me and The Desk, The Desk knows what we must write. Me and The Desk are working closely here . . .

[Wolf leans forwards again, cheek on the desk, listening for voices, listening for stories, fingers tapping the desk surface gently, tap, tap, tap.]

Mrs Death:
Wolfie! Have you got any spaghetti seeds?

Wolf:
Spaghetti seeds?

Mrs Death:
You forgot to plant spaghetti seeds! I'm hungry! What are we doing for lunch? We need to grow some spaghetti! Wolfie, what is wrong with you? . . . Wolfie, what are you writing about now?

Wolf:
I am writing about . . . I am typing up everything you say to me, Mrs Death . . . I am waiting for you to give me another story like Tilly Tuppence. I am typing everything you say . . . *Spaghetti seeds! What is wrong with you?*

Mrs Death:
Really? Are you typing this?

Wolf:
Yep. I just typed: *Really? Are you typing this?*

Mrs Death:
Well, what do you want to know?

Wolf:
Well, what do you want to know?

What do you mean, *What do you want to know?* Mrs Death, I want to know you. I want to know everything about Death and you, Mrs Death, at least everything you want me to know so I can write about you. I must admit I haven't ghost-written a book before. Ha, that's funny, I'm ghost-writing a book for Mrs Death, I'll use that later . . . note to self.

Anyway, I think this is more a case of what you want to tell me about you, what you want to share about your um . . . life . . . What is your process? Do you have a process? Is there a system? How do you decide who lives and who dies? How does it feel to be you? When did you start being Death? Why are you 'Mrs'? Have you been married? Who does Death love? Give me a scoop, tell me a secret, have you got any love interests right now? When did you get

inside this desk? I dunno, I have a million questions . . .
Let's start somewhere easy . . .

Question one: Mrs Death, do dead people go to their own
funerals?

Mrs Death:
[Mrs Death slowly peels another smelly boiled egg.]

Oh no! I hate funerals. Are you going to write about funerals?
Urghhhh!

You ask me: Do dead people go to their own funerals? Of
course they do, but not in the way you're thinking, not how
it is in the movies. They don't stand at the back, invisible,
smiling and waiting for living people to say nice things
about them. They don't stand in the wake watching who is
scoffing the egg sandwiches and who is grabbing after their
money in the will or who is making advances on their widow.
They don't really care who is at the graveside or not. The
dead have no interest in shit poems about how sad the living
are when they die. If they did, there would be an uproar!
Shit eulogies! What is it the living always say at funerals?
He had a good innings! What does that even mean? Innings?

Funerals are mostly for the living and not the dead. Funerals
are ritual and letting go and saying goodbye. Dead people
are at their funerals in spirit, in connection, in the shape

of love. And no, they don't care if the stale egg sandwiches are served on paper plates and not the good china. They don't care if you cannot afford a nice new black suit. They don't care if you cannot cry. Mostly they want to be remembered in your heart, they want to be remembered how they lived and not how they died. Wolf, are you writing a book about funerals? Are you sure anyone would want to read that? Bit dreary, don't you think? A book of funerals. That's a bit bleak, isn't it? Which funerals will you write about? The funeral of the People's Princess and the pauper's funeral? I mean, picture me now: I'm in a bookshop in 2025.

[Mrs Death clicks her fingers. The attic room is transformed into Shakespeare and Co in Paris. Wolf is transported there, bewildered, baffled and thrilled. Wolf spins around, mouth wide open. It really is the most beautiful bookshop in the world . . .]

Look! Here you are, here is the debut book by Wolf: *Mrs Death Misses Death.* Oh, OK, nice cover! A shocking sexy picture of Mrs Death looking a bit Grace Jones and gothic, sinister but smoking hot. Love the cover. No, I really do. I have no clothes on. The perspective is mad. They think I am at least nine feet tall. But I am black and beautiful. Actually it is utterly sexist and misogynoir, but I guess a sexy image of a towering black Goddess version of Mrs Death will sell books. I get it. I am so sick and tired of the black hood and scythe thing . . . moving on . . . OK, I am opening the book and the first chapter is . . . really? Princess

Diana? A picture of Diana, dead Diana, Princess Diana with her coffin and a million mourners, it is London and it is raining with flowers and wreaths and weeping poor people. *Alas! Too young! Too sad! Too soon! Her sons! Too tragic!* Now next page. No name! Ah chapter two, a picture of a cardboard box, look at the dead homeless girl with no money to be dead and buried, and look how she dies without dignity in rags, in a piss-stained sleeping bag with a plastic bag for a pillow in the lonely pissing rain, all alone. Ooh the contradiction! Who do we grieve for? Who gets a hashtag on Twitter? Who makes the front page? Who makes us more sad? Do we cry for the princess or weep for the pauper? *Oh the princess! Oh the peasant!* Oh for crying out loud, this is a bizarre book, Wolf . . . Not. Very. Cheerful. Thank you not very much! No! Stop it! Stop it! Stop it!

Wolf:
Stop it! Stop it! Stop it! Stop it!

[The room spins and changes back to Wolf's attic room. Wolf is rocking in the wooden chair, typing stop it, stop it, stop it and screaming stop it stop it stop it, pages and pages of stop it. stop it. stop it.]

Stop it! Stop it! Stop it!

Mrs Death:
[She peels another boiled egg and starts to eat it.]

Stop it! Stop it! Stop it! Stop it! Give up! It's no good, give up, Wolf, give up, give up, give up, stop, before it is too late, it's earlier than you think. Give up, give up, give up, it's earlier than you think, Wolf! Give up and write something cheerful instead. People have enough misery in their lives. Humans like happy stories full of laughter and colour, not stories about dead people and their dreary funerals and people crying all over the place! The people want laughter! I want laughter!

Wolf:
People laugh at funerals. I laugh at funerals. Lots of people laugh at funerals. Laughing at death is natural: we laugh in grief, we laugh out of disbelief, we laugh with love, I suppose, and sorrow and shock. I laughed at my mother's funeral. I am laughing now. HA HA HA.

[Wolf laughs a big fake laugh. Wolf rolls and then lights a fag. There is an awkward silence, and they continue talking . . .]

Pooh! . . . Those eggs you eat stink. Why are you always eating eggs?

Mrs Death:
I eat an egg when a new egg is made. It's all about eggs. Life makes eggs. Death eats eggs. Circle of life and death. It is way more complex than that, but for now, all you need to know is that it is all about one word: eggs.

Do you have any salt?

Wolf:
Salt?

Mrs Death:
Second word you need to know: salt.

There is salt in all living things, Wolf. There is salt in death. There is salt in tears, sweat, sperm, juice, piss, blood. Life is salt. Death is salty too. Sea salt, the sea and the land, the peat, and salt in the air and the volcano and the sulphur and the flame and the world goes on, with salt and eggs, eggs and salt. Circle of life and death. I eat an egg. My sister Life lays an egg. So I have to eat more eggs. Salt and eggs, eggs and salt.

It is hard to keep up with her, to be honest. My sister. Life. She is an over-achiever, little Miss Abundance. My sister! Imagine growing up with that, with her for a sister! Just imagine if Life was your sister! Eggy little goody two-shoes eggy fart face. The earth would be horribly over-crowded if I didn't eat her eggs and destroy her spawn and do my job efficiently. She is constantly vomiting, and puking cherry pips and cherry blossom everywhere. Every time Life lays an egg, Death eats an egg. All who come from eggs are connected, every creature, every egg, every mammal and fish and insect. Eggs. Salt. Birth. Blood. Death. And on and on it goes, never ending . . . eggy eggs eggy eggs . . . What came first, the chicken or the egg? Life came first! She always comes first! Ha! Selfish fish fishy eggy fart face.

[Snaps her fingers.]

Ha! I know what's funny! Monkeys are funny! Wolf, why don't you write a book about a monkey instead? In my humble opinion there were never enough books about monkeys. Shakespeare never wrote a thing about monkeys. Bearded idiot! Monkeys are hilarious, monkeys eating bananas, funny monkeys, cheeky monkeys, funny monkeys on typewriters, funny monkeys riding bicycles. I love monkeys: write that for me. I'd like to read a lovely funny monkey book. Everyone loves monkeys . . . Come on.

Clean page, type this, write this down, I'll help you:

The Monkey Book by Wolf Willeford. Once upon a time there was a big beautiful monkey, he was far, far away from home. He grew up to be a huge and powerful black gorilla but he lived in a zoo and . . .

Wolf:
And let me guess, his name was Harambe and he was shot?

Mrs Death, monkeys are highly intelligent and sensitive creatures. I saw a nature programme recently with David

Attenborough, and there was a death in a group of monkeys. I was in floods of tears watching it, I mean, it was harrowing. Monkeys are affected by death, trauma and grief just like humans, they show empathy and remorse. A family of monkeys feel loss when they lose a member of their group. They gather together and hug each other, just as we humans do, I mean like human beings do. If you want me to write about monkeys I'll write about that, I'll write about Mrs Death and the dead gorilla! The killing of Harambe! Why did they kill Harambe? Why don't we respect and save the animals, Mrs Death? What will we do when the last elephants are extinct, Mrs Death? Who will save the turtles and the coral reefs and the rainforests? Who will help us save the natural world when Attenborough dies, Mrs Death? Mrs Death? Can you answer me?

Mrs Death:
No. Can't be bothered.

Wolf:
Wow, really? You? Death? Can't be bothered? Mrs Death, you stink my room up with the smell of eggs, eggs, eggs. Don't you have a village to flood, a plane to crash, a bomb to drop . . . or are you here just to distract and torture me? I think I want to be alone, you are annoying me now.

Mrs Death:
Oh come on, there's no need to be like that, Wolfie. After

all, you're sitting at my desk. You asked for this, you summoned me, remember that, I literally come with the furniture . . . I'm afraid as long as you sit and write and worship at my desk, you're stuck with me.

Besides, I don't annoy you, it isn't me. I don't torture you: you torture yourself. I watch you. You think about one thing you did wrong, something you said, or a time you put your foot in it, and then you replay it, the same moment over and over in your hot curly head, getting more and more anxious with each replay. You are a catastrophist and your moods swing violently. You make things up! You gather memories of times you failed or you were overlooked or you were thoughtless or clumsy, times you could have done better, times you said something wrong or made a mistake or forgot your manners, and you join them together. You do this, catastrophising, over and over on a loop until you have a cluster of things to cringe about and then you sit and loathe yourself as all these tiny (un)remarkable events play on and on in a vicious circle in your head, all adding up to one juicy sandwich of self-loathing anxiety. It's quite hard work in your head, Wolf, I've been in there and you torture yourself, you panic, you waste your time, you waste energy, you worry needlessly, all on your own. You berate and distract yourself, you give yourself a hard time, you tell yourself this is not enough, that you are not enough. You know what, Wolf? You are enough.

Wolf:
Thank you.

Mrs Death . . . I don't want to give up.

Mrs Death:
Darling, are you scared?

Wolf:
Scared of what?

Mrs Death:
Are you scared that if you write this book you will get too close to me and . . .

Wolf:
And . . .
Die?

Mrs Death:
Yes, do you think that all this Mrs Death talk will lead you to your own death?

Wolf:
Death isn't catching.

Mrs Death:
But has it crossed your mind that if you talk with me every

day you draw your own death closer, no or yes or no or yes or . . .

Wolf:

No . . . and yes and no. Well. Yes. Actually yes, now you mention it. Yes. And no. I am aware that by talking about death that I am thinking about death and pulling death towards me by even writing this but I won't give up. I'm inspired and I'm honoured you guide me to write your stories. We are all going to die one day, right, if there is one thing I have learned from you so far, it is that we are all going to die one day. And so I think this book can be a celebration of you, of the female spirit of death. Mrs Death, you're amazing. I mean, why haven't they written about you before? You are Death, you are the Grim Reaper, the shadow keeper, the mother of Otherland, the caretaker of all souls, the black angel of eternal night, the shepherdess of the long sleep, the grand madam of eternity, the Goddess of the night, the lightkeeper of the long goodbye, you are the night nurse, the siren of the deep black lullaby, the shadow of the moon and the mother that blows out the candle of life and . . .

Mrs Death:

Hahaha! Is that how you want to depict me, like Florence Nightingale, lady with the lamp, softly blowing the candle out, nighty night, sleep tight, time to die?

Wolf:

What? No. You're definitely not a Florence Nightingale. Not in my book anyway. But sometimes you miss, Mrs Death, sometimes you miss and people live against the odds; sometimes people dodge your bullet, sometimes you . . . You let people go, you let people live, you let people in, or is it out? I get confused . . . but sometimes you allow it, you give people more time or a second chance. I have seen you. I mean, I have watched and observed the world and I have imagined it is you, Mrs Death, nudging a child out of the way of busy traffic. You are that invisible hand on a shoulder pulling someone back from the edge. I have seen plants come back to life. I have seen you strike but miss and then retreat. How do people survive? I believe it was you who pushed people out of the windows of the World Trade Center on September 11th, Mrs Death, was this to try and save their lives? I believe it was you who threw people overboard on the *Titanic* to swim to life boats. I believe you hold dinghies filled with fleeing immigrants afloat on rough seas. I think you give as much as you take. I mean, who else is always first on the scene of a hurricane or tsunami or terrorist attack, who else? You, Mrs Death, you give and you take. I need to understand why you sometimes let people have enough hope to live . . . For example, the fire, that fire, my mother, you let me live, I saw you, there must be a reason I'm here.

Mrs Death:

Wolf, I never left you. I remember you, your bare feet in your pyjamas, smoke and chaos, you howling up at me, all that rage. I remember all that happened the night of the fire . . . You stayed with me. You were lucky to survive. I didn't save you, your mother's strength did that: your mum, she woke you and got you out of the building in time . . . *Can you smell smoke?* Remember, she shook you awake . . . *Run*, she said, remember?

Wolf:

Please help me write your story.

Mrs Death:

Alright then, let me help you. Are you sitting comfortably?

Type this, Wolf.

Wolf:

Type this, Wolf.

OK. Ready . . .

Mrs Death:

The birth of Death: my life started like Life, my life started with love, with love and breath and blood. I was in the dark, in deep hibernation, burrowed down in the underneath where the roots begin and the earth is black and wet. It is silent down there, under the underneath. It's dark too, dark as the womb, dark as a tomb. It takes all your eyes wide open to see there is nothing to see but the darkest dark, but you get used to it after a while. Death was born there. I was born.

I am always there, out of the corner of your eye in some far-off field. Death is there, a fleeting moment on the edge of time, there, darting in the hedgerows, chewing on plump cowslips and blackberries.

Not many people know this but . . . Death is a rabbit.

[*Int. Wolf's room. Mrs Death begins to shrink and morph and change into a white china rabbit sitting on the desk. The rabbit shines, it has a pink nose and painted eyelashes. There is one person in the room. The writer called Wolf is sitting and drinking all alone. Wolf sits slumped at the antique desk, a mop of curly hair, hunched over, whispering and muttering to a white china rabbit. There are eggshells scattered all over the attic floor.*]

Death Is a Rabbit

death is a rabbit
darting in a distant field
death is the stranger
you feed at your door
death is the cherry blossom
the sweet and the sour
death is a rabbit
leaping through long dewy grass
in a far-off field
seen from your train view
out of the tail of your eye
run rabbit, run, run
death is the stranger
sharing your sweet cherry wine
and hot rabbit stew.

Mrs Death and Her Lover Time

Once upon a time, a very long time ago, in the time before all of this began — in the beginning and before the here and the now — the Moon and the Sun agreed to make Time the boss so they would both know the time. They needed Time so neither one would have more time to shine than the other. With Time in charge the Sun and the Moon would know how fast to go and how slow; from summer to winter, from day to night. How else would the Sun know when to rise? How else does the Moon know it is midnight? How else would they know when to eclipse each other and dance in each other's light and shadow? Time knows.

Time is wise. Time has much less to do with the human idea of straight lines and itineraries and diaries and budgets and schedules and everything to do with circles and cycles and colour and light and sound. Time is forever. Time lives in space. Time is in time with the echo of your heartbeat drumming: *dum-dum dum-dum dum-dum*.

I was doing Time. Time was doing me. At the beginning of time, Time and Death were great lovers and quite a handsome pair. I met Time sometime and next thing I know Time is all mine and Time is so beautiful and it is a beautiful time and when we were together time stopped and we were timeless. How time flies when you're having fun.

Time was my first love. Time felt reliable, solid, like a tree with strong roots that go all the way down to the centre of the heart of the earth and with arms that can go all around the universe. All that Time, it greases the cogs that make the earth spin on its axis. Time is very hands-on. Time touches people, holds them in the one place. Time tells people where they are and how long it is necessary for them to be there and why. It is very hard to move or grow when you are living by rules ruled by Time and age and years; it is a very controlling experience when you realise how much of everything is governed by Time.

Time has an eye that looks as though it is made of a mirror. It reflects all that is here and there and past and future. If you stop and face Time, take a deep breath, you'll find your own reflection in that eye. It is then you'll see who you were and who you are and then you'll see who you want to be. Often you'll find that you were never moving forward or looking backward, but you were always just in one place, inside you, and here, the place we call the present. I don't blame anyone for falling for the tricks of Time. Intoxicating. Hypnotising. You fall under Time's gaze, swim, then get pulled into a time-warp. The machinery is in your dreams and intentions. You must stop running. Stop still and look Time in the eye and face yourself and see who you really always were, who you really are beneath all that rush rush, hurry hurry, busy busy.

I spent thousands of years under Time's watchful eye. We lived in that rocky bed. I was barefoot in a cave, swimming in volcanic lava, back when Time was young. We were all young then, I suppose. The world was young, planet earth was all fire and volcanos and meteor showers.

When I look into the eye of Time, I see it all. Together, we see everything, the purpose of this, and why I must do what I do and who I do: the meaning of the work of Death. What happens when Death looks Time in the eye? What happens when Time and Death meet face to face? What happens when Time and Mrs Death make love? I look Time in the eye. Time stops and looks Death in the eye. We hold that moment and fall through it, and things explode, then there we have it all, the thread that tugs us and pulls us together. When Time and Death have a fuck, Time has the end of the thread, Death comes with the finish. Time calls Time. Are we friends? *Yes and no.* Lovers? *Well, it's complicated.*

Truth is, our jobs are a strain on our relationship. For example: you saw what happened to the dinosaurs. That was the end of our first fling and our first big fight. A conflict of eggs and ego and self-interest and sulphur and BOOM!

Time keeps Time. Time is inside the ebb and flow and the wax and wane. The time of the month, the tides of Time. Time is a demagogue dictator. Time is a capitalist. Time is a tricky trickster. Time is a charming fellow. Time isn't easy to hold on to, to stop and talk to, to sit with. Time takes time. Time takes Time seriously. Time walks with a wooden stick, a tall staff, *tap, tap, tap*, everywhere Time goes. If you stop and listen carefully you can hear Time, *tick tock tap; tick tock tap*, you hear Time ahead of you, passing you and then behind you. Time sneaks up on us, Time sneaks past and then disappears into the fogs of Time.

Time carries our dreams – billions of years, billions of stories and memories in clay jars. When humans sleep, tiny grains from these jars fall in your eyelashes to make sleeping sand. When you have a very real and vivid dream it is a grain from these jars of Time, grains of Time, of memory, of your fate, of your past, present and future. It's so vital and so important to listen to your dreams; to try to remember to write them down if you can. Dreams are messages from you to you, from old you to new you, things your ancestors and your DNA have stored in the jars of Time.

Why, how the years have flown! one says, and tears fill the eyes, soft sentimental tears. How we yearn and long and wish for Time to stop, to capture a moment, to stay in one sweet spot. It seems one day you are only nine and it's all a big adventure. Then you are nineteen and it is all ahead of you. And then suddenly you are twenty-nine and you laugh at how you know you should know better. And then you are thirty-nine and you are still laughing and acting surprised by where you are. And then if you are lucky one day all of a sudden you are fifty-nine and sixty-nine and then suddenly you are . . .

You. You are always you inside there.

To grow old is a great gift; it is the best of gifts. And when you grow old well, it is constantly nearly Christmas . . . constantly ticking. Listen for it, *tick tock tap, tick tock tap*. Oh, your teeth and knees; you'll miss your teeth and your knees. And your hair. You will miss your beautiful hair. And not being tired. You'll miss not always being tired. You'll miss having plenty of Time. Inside you, all that Time inside you. You laugh and cry and feel like you: inside you, you are you. Inside the rooms of your head are all the times of you. You laugh like you always did. You have some of the same dreams and visit those castles and forests and those strange rooms you only inhabit in your dream world. That won't change. Even if you are old now, you can still always fly in your dreams. You may still have some of the same fears and doubts: you are the same, but changed, but you.

In the English language when people die the mourners often say, *Oh it was their Time* and Time gets all the credit. And they also say, *Time heals* and again Time takes the glory and I am not having that! And when people die too young or too early, well, again it is Time the human focuses on: how long did they live, how long did they have? Time this and Time that, and we clash and fight over that too. There is a strange love and hate between Time and Death. But a long time ago, back when the world was very young and just evolving, Time gave me gifts, Time gave me space. Time gave me something to work with: the notion of passing, of life passing through to Death's deadline. In return I gave Time something to work against, something to run from or work to. The beginning and the ending that is never-ending. Death and Time are doing a similar job when you look at us closely. We are as close as we can be without my sister Life popping up and demanding attention and demanding we all have the time of her life.

Lifetime. Life. Time. Life will sing gaily to me, *You see, it's an actual phrase. The human will say 'time of death' for a reason, a human being will have only one 'time of death', just once, but they can have a life time all the time, life, time, time of their lives all their life! See, it's all about the phrasing, it's all down to the phrasing,* says my sister joyfully, whilst pushing cherry blossom petals out of her tear ducts so they rain down all pretty all over Japan. *Sakura!* Life sings, *Sakura! Time of your life!*

Life is tied to Time. Time consumes Life. Time and Life are lovers on an ongoing seesaw for all of our lifetimes. It is a long love they share that goes too fast. By all accounts they are very happy together. Life is all about Time and Time is all about Life. I go along with it. I smile, I nod, I say nothing. If there is one thing I know, Death knows everything has a natural end. Life is so lively, it's her nature. Life forgets Time has a relationship with Death. But how would Life be Life if she spent all her time with Time worrying about Death and the relationship of Time and Death? See? Life is Life, why should Life care that Death does Time and Time does Death? Death counts on Time. Time loves a deadline: a dead line. Time loves some finality; my cold and clean finish. Life believes Time is for Life, that Time is for the living. Life is most comfortable living in denial and refusing to believe that Time and Death must also have some sort of love for each other.

Temporicide: a good word. It means to kill time.

I roll the word around my mouth. I imagine killing Time once and for all. Can Death kill Time? What would this world be like without Time? Would the Sun crash into the Moon? Would the sea rise and rise and flood the earth? Is this what is happening now? Is this how the world ends? The death of Time, a slow dripping sound, the melting of ice, the water rising, every day higher and higher. The water, carving through rock and seeping into land, everywhere a lake, then a sea, and the human develops gills and returns to the salt and water and darkness.

Time is subtle. Time is the greatest artist. What an artist is Time: look at the sculptures Time makes of human faces, the carvings Time makes with our feelings, the paintings of our life journeys in our heart's song. Human faces are the greatest art of Time.

Harder, Time cries.
Faster, Time cries.
Slower, Time cries,
More, more, more
Time sings

But live, damn it, live.
Live awake and live alive
And take your Time.
Take your
Time.

The Desk: Mrs Death's Office

In Mrs Death's office the printer sometimes gets jammed. You must understand the problems this can cause. The machine runs out of ink, the pages get stuck together and the numbers repeat.

Somewhere, somebody dies on an operating table. The surgeon wipes his brow and takes off his mask. He sighs heavily and says, *We lost him* . . . There is a long pause filled with the weight of failure and loss.

But just then the body jolts and appears to come back to life. *Bleeeep. Bleeeep.* The heart beats, there is a steady pulse, the drama is over. The doctors and the nurses and everybody in the theatre cheer and cry. They wipe a tear and pat the surgeon on the back. *Well done.* A huge sigh of relief and congratulations and . . . then just as suddenly . . . the patient jolts twice more and then flatlines and dies all over again. This time for good. The patient is really gone this time.

Dead. Twice. Life came and went. Mrs Death was there twice that same day. Do you think that's intentional? Do you think Mrs Death does this on purpose? No. Mrs Death is a very busy lady. No, believe me, that is a jammed printer. Mrs Death's system has a system.

It is man-made machines that make errors to torment humans.

Mrs Death in Holloway Prison

Say Her Name: For Sarah Reed, Black Lives Matter

Sarah suffered
Sarah was falsely arrested
for shoplifting in Regent Street
the policeman was seen on CCTV
dragging Sarah by her hair
while punching her
repeatedly in the face
his name was PC James Kiddie
he was subject to a number
of previous complaints
PC Kiddie was a liability
a tragedy waiting to happen
Sarah suffered
mental health issues
ever since the sudden death

of her newborn baby
Sarah suffered
severe mental ill-health
she was detained
under Section 3 of
the Mental Health Act
Sarah suffered
a sexual assault in
Maudsley Hospital
south London
Sarah suffered
Sarah was a victim
of an attempted rape
she fought off her attacker
and injured him
the staff called the police
Sarah was arrested
Sarah suffered
Sarah was ill
trapped in the
justice system
without medical help
however
throughout her time
on remand
Sarah never received
any medication
Sarah suffered

then on the
11th January 2016
the Reed family
received a phone call
from Holloway Prison
informing them
that Sarah was dead
they were told that
Sarah had strangled herself
whilst lying on her bed
the prison staff said
she strangled herself
they offered
no comfort
or compassion
the family were refused
the right to see the body of Sarah
the family of Sarah Reed
are still desperate
to know what happened
Sarah was buried on
Monday 8th February 2016
in a private family ceremony
say her name
Sarah Reed
suffered.

Mrs Death: Marsha and Martha

Edinburgh, 31st December, 1788

Martha and Marsha or Marsha and Martha, depending which you knew best or more or less. They were identical twins. Totally and utterly identical to look at but polar opposites to speak to, for one was good and one was bad; one was gentle, and one was mad and wild; one had a temper and the other quite kind and mild. But more to the point, one was dead and one was alive. Martha and Marsha, Marsha and Martha, but you see, one was dead and one was alive.

It's all my fault: I never knew which was which.

You could not tell them apart, they were inseparable, always in the room at the same time, but in another way not, for one was very dead and the other very alive. But which was which? I couldn't tell. I really didn't know who was who, and now, writing this down, I believe they did not know: nobody knew. Not even they knew, who was here and who was there, they did not know, not really. Martha and Marsha or Marsha and Martha: which one was alive and which one was dead? It troubles me to this day. Because if they didn't know, and I didn't know, then it was as if they were both here and not here, both dead and both alive.

It is New Year's Eve. Marsha is fixing her hair in the mirror. Or was it Martha? I don't know. For now and for the sake of this telling, let's call this young lady Marsha. Marsha. Marsha. She is so vainglorious about her hair, a mane of gorgeous curly hair, the colour of chestnuts in sunlight. She is dressing her hair with pomade and a perfume of sandalwood pervades the bedroom. She sits and twists her hair in her fingers and places her curls at her temple. She has perfect golden-brown ringlets and black pearl studs in her ears. I am watching. I watch her now and she is sitting at her dressing table in formal evening dress — she wears an exquisite and delicate gown of white lace and pale pink velvet. A silver locket with a rabbit engraved on the front around her throat. She looks into her green eyes, they sparkle, lively in her olive face. She dusts the soft brown skin with rose powder, adds rose oil behind each ear, and she is finally ready for the ball.

There is a draught, the candles flicker, the blue embroidered curtains move and suddenly there behind her in the mirror is her twin Martha. Let's call this one Martha. Naughty Martha, bad Martha. She grins at her sister in the mirror. It is a monster of a grin, a mania, her head jolts like a puppet. Her bright green eyes shine and spin in their red sockets. She sticks out her tongue, licks her lips and then she pops out her left breast from her bodice and bounces a tit on the palm of her hand. She cavorts, swinging from side to side, her fat brown breast bouncing obscenely. She pinches her nipple and licks her own lips and laughs and laughs and laughs. Downstairs the guests are arriving, the band are playing, the beautiful and the damned. Marsha and Martha descend down the grand oak staircase to the Hogmanay ball. And all of Edinburgh society are there, guests of the Lord Willeford's mansion all gaze and look upwards at his newest acquisitions, identical twins, girl slaves, Martha and Marsha. Murmuring from the gathered guests below:

I hear he taught these wild savages to read and write!

Well, I never!

Don't they look exotic!

And to this day I still don't know why one lives. To this day I do not know which one missed death, and how could I, how dare I, Mrs Death, miss death?

Wolf: The Vanishing

They found your clothes on the beach
we all assumed you'd swum out of reach
they found your shoes side by side
your phone and keys tucked inside

we blame ourselves, we blame the deep cruel sea
you swam away and now you are free
they found your clothes folded neat
you leave this world, your story incomplete

I've imagined you, salt water in your lungs
sand in your mouth, crabs feed on your tongue
and you wash up bloated blue
oh we all cry, we all cry for you

without a trace, you disappear
leaving all you love and all you fear
you dissolve out of choice
I phone your answer machine to hear your voice

you turn a page, you make a fresh start
you hardly notice, you break my heart
they found your clothes folded neat
you leave this world, your story is complete

I don't blame you, I blame the deep cruel sea
I blame this world, how it's been hurting me
you leave the past on the shore
I give, you give and take no more

Wolf: The Vanishing

Wolf writes to Wolf's father

'A member of the public contacted officers fearing someone may have gone into the water. The caller found a pile of clothing folded neatly on the sand, but could not see anyone in the area whom the garments belonged to. A search of the beach was carried out by the local police supported by the dog unit and Coastguard, but no one has been found.'

Ramsgate Herald – April 2008

Dear Dad,

You once told Mum that you'd disappear and that we'd never hear from you ever again. You were drunk. You said that one day you'd walk out of our front door and just never turn back. You laughed. It seemed an odd thing to say, a cruel thing to say. Like you were trying to hurt us. I remember you were laughing, it was a cold laughter. I recall looking up and hearing Mum – her laugh was empty. She said, *Don't be ridiculous,* but her eyes were welling up. You were both so pissed. I didn't know what that all meant, and I didn't believe it then, but I believe it now.

It's all our fault, of course, we take the blame. We probably took too much, we asked too much and it drained you and you drained yourself and drained us all. You drank too much. You both did. Those early years are heavy with burden, they are made of a thick and dense material. I was only about five, maybe six years old, but I remember parts of it. Your depression, how the darkness ate everything and how it ate us all up. Mum told me you were haunted by unwanted thoughts. I understand that now: unwanted thoughts. I have unwanted thoughts, Dad. I don't want these thoughts and these dark impulses, and I wonder if I inherited this from you, Dad? Were you bipolar? I wonder if we were the same and if we could have maybe saved each other.

Nobody knows this but once, when I was around fourteen, I said suddenly to Old Man Willeford that I wanted to die. I think I was trying to shock him. I think I wanted his help. I think I wanted him to see me. I know I wanted to be like you, Dad, and I was trying to understand what this sad black hole was inside me. But now all I remember is how angry this statement made Grandpa Willeford. I remember how he twisted and grabbed me and held me out of the window of the building. His face was spit and fury.

Shall I let you go? he yelled. *Is this what you want? Do you want to die? Do you?* I struggled and reached for his sports jacket lapels. Grandpa tipped me upside down and out of the window. All the blood rushing to my head, the traffic, the city all swirling, spinning, all upside down and miles below. For just two or three moments I went limp as if to prepare to fly and fall. Grandpa froze and I froze. I scared myself how willing I was, how willing we both were to let me go. He hated me. I hated him. And he hated that Mum was dead and he was left to look after me. I know I reminded him of his daughter but all wrong and not girl enough. And not boy enough either. But then I lurched and panicked and kicked and grabbed at Grandpa's arms and shoulders and jacket, I was clawing for dear life. I could have died then. Grandpa could have accidentally lost his grip and I would have fallen to certain death, but he suddenly yanked me back in.

That was a powerful moment. For both of us. For two or three seconds I wanted him to let go. Smack. Crunch. I would've crashed onto the pavement ten floors below. My head smashing open like a melon on the concrete pavement. All of the people, our neighbours below screaming at the mess of my bloodied body. But then Grandpa would be a murderer. I said I wanted to die, not I wanted to be murdered, and there is a difference, isn't there? I didn't want to be killed. I wanted to kill myself. It's different: it is about choice. But these thoughts of dying, of killing myself, I still have them, I just don't talk about them or try to act on them so often.

Dad, you always said we were all cunts. That was your favourite word. You would get drunk and say that I was a cunt. *You cunt*, you'd say to me. *You cunt.* You said Mum was a cunt. We were all cunts. You said you could never decide who was the biggest cunt. But in the end, one by one, you left me like a cunt. You all left me. Do I die like this, by being buried alive in all of your shit and abandonment? Just a thought – an unwanted thought. It was always so good of you to remember to tell us we were cunts.

You'd be furious at the television and shout, *Cunt!* You'd lecture me on how someone was a specific type of cunt, constantly referring to your ever-growing list of cunts. How they tried to fuck us over, our world, our family. People were gonna fuck you, fuck you up or fuck us over. All you knew is that they were some cunt from the old days, who treated a cunt like a cunt for being cunts in the first cunting place.

Once we were in a café and Mum waved to say hello to someone. And you snapped and said, *Hello cunt! You cunty person from the cunting past.* And suddenly you got very cross and shouted *Cunts!* You spat and threw your cup and smashed it into a thousand pieces. You tipped the table over in the middle of the café, plates went flying as egg and chips and tea splattered the floors and walls. All the café all staring with judging and hateful eyes and you were seething and screaming for the whole café to hear:

Cunts! Don't you know they are cunts? They are all cunts! Cunts!!

I remember being hungry as a kid. How Mum shared out a tin of beans on toast for tea. No money for the meter. You and Mum smoking roll-ups made out of fag butts. Sometimes we had no heat, no hot water. Nothing. We had this big cold city and what little we did have was ours and our own invention. But I look back now and love us. You were too young to cope, too young to be parents, too young to fend for yourselves. We three were lost cunts, my mum and dad and me. I look at a photo of us, you and Mum were teenagers. Too young to have a baby. You did not know how beautiful you were. You apologised constantly – *Sorry* – but you kept drinking. *Sorry*, you'd say, and then you let the Devil in to spoil things and then you said *Sorry* again and apologised to those cunts for being cunts to you. I remember the vultures and the predators, the dealers and the cunts. I remember the smell. Stale smoke and cheap lager and whisky. I don't remember everything, I was too young, but I remember flashes: the noise and the smoke and the tinny music and how things felt dirty and ashy, chewed up and eaten up, swallowed down and pushed under. All used up. Used like cunts.

This is my message in a bottle to you now: stick some of this time in your pocket, just for us. Keep something just for yourself, Dad. Don't give it all away. Don't give everything to the Devil and the cunts because they are actually cunts and they cannot help themselves but use people like cunts.

Dad, as I write this, I daydream that you're alive out there somewhere. You swam away. You vanished and disappeared. I grieve for you as though you have died, I cry, you just stopped being my dad, stopped living in your version of here and then. You are free now. You are alive in another universe. I suppose you stopped living a lie. I like to imagine you started anew, you threw the old you away and you changed your name.

They found your clothes on the beach.

The world was such hard work for you, fighting your demons, your unwanted thoughts, unwanted chaos, unwanted child, unwanted wife, unwanted everything. Constantly fighting and holding grudges and burning bridges and keeping a list of cunts. I think we're all cunts. All of us. Me included. I kinda miss you, I miss you telling me what a cunt I am. If I could, I would tell you how I am a big and grown-up cunt now. *Look at me now*, I'd say, *I'm a big cunt.*

You are not dead — you are just far away and elsewhere, changing and ageing and growing old. How is that for you, are you a fat cunt in glasses now? Are you a grey cunt or a bald cunt?

I live alone and I look after myself now. I will be twenty-one soon. I want to be a real writer one day. I practise and write every day. Books are my friends. Dreams are my real life. Sometimes I dream of us and we are together again, me and my mum and you, Dad. We are all in that tiny flat on the 17th floor, and I wake up crying, with a pain in my chest and weight on me. I cry. As I write this, I cry. This is a letter for you, Dad, a message in a bottle that I will throw into the green sea. Wherever you are, if you read this, I am sorry and I am not sorry. I just hope you found peace and love and the best of the cunts.

With love, Wolf xx

Mrs Death: Sun Kill Son

Australia, 1978

Three people have died
and a teenage boy is missing
after their vehicle broke down
in the outback, Australia
police say the bodies of two adults
and their four-year-old son
were found south of Darwin
a search is now under way
for the thirteen-year-old boy
the bodies were found
sun-fried and torn open
police say the bodies
looked like
torn open
barbecued

bloody
sun-dried
steak tomatoes
the teenager appears
to have wandered off
in extreme weather
police suspect
the thirteen-year-old boy
murdered
and then tore
them open
and ate the
internal organs
of everyone in the car
then left the vehicle
like a fucking mental case
police are right
to be fucking concerned
because temperatures
in that region
have exceeded
fucking 45°C
in recent fucking days
fucking hell
that is fucking hot
according to Australia's
fucking Bureau of
fucking Meteorology

that is as fucking hot
as a fucking freshly fucked fox
in a fucking bush fucking fire
confirmed fucking
Northern fucking Territory
fucking Police
fuck

Mrs Death: Mother's Milk

Mrs Death's recurring dream

I dream
I lie on my side
my belly is round
the baby is still in my arms
I kiss each tiny perfect finger

I feel love for the child
I want to feel it latch
on to my breast
I feel a rush of love
waves and waves of love
real and absolute love

A love I have heard
other women speak of
a love mothers boast about
a love that death will never end

I feel it
As if it is real
I understand the bond
Of mother and child
I recall the heat of life in my arms
the weight, the smell of the baby
the quiet milky light

And because
this is just a dream
the baby is laughing
and then talking
and then walking
towards me
and my time

It's a lovely thing
alive and beautiful
curly hair
big grey eyes
just like yours
my love
forever
like Time

We name the child
breath and heart
and Wolf
and it is
Wolf

Running towards us
with outstretched arms
I see Wolf now
running towards us
alive and spirit and free

I jolt upright and
wake up to see the sun rising
the morning bright and vivid
as the love I felt in my dream
the love I still feel now as I write this

In my dream I felt love
a love that Death
could never break
a love for you
my love, my love
my love for you and
this world, this day and this
Time, this short time we share

The love I felt
in my dream
was so true
this morning
I forgive my mistake
my accidents and losses
the things that could never be
this morning for once
all is quiet inside me

There is love
as I write this
it is banging in my heart
and hurting in my chest
this life is love, Life is love

Time misses Death
Time Mrs Death
calling Time, Mrs Death
Time misses
Mrs Death
Time.

Mrs Death: The Moors

the undercover policeman / had *Sunblest* written on his chest
/ as he knocked on doors / you made the tea / with grave
dirt / under your nails / from the moors / you said *no* /
try next door instead / as the copper stepped inside / again
you said *no* / you said *no no no* / *we don't take Sunblest bread*
/ *we take Mothers Pride* / Myra you lied and / you tore at
mother's pride / and you said Ian Brady turned your peroxide
head / and after that first kill / you told us Ian made you
scrub the spade / scrub that grave dirt / from the moors
/ then you two watched TV / and cuddled in bed / he
said / *young children are more likely to go with a lady for a ride in*
a car / you said Ian needed you / and you said you needed
to be needed / so you stayed with him / and together you
tore at mother's pride / you tore / and you tear and / grab
excuses / grab at straws / blame the media blame Ian Brady
/ for what you both did on the moors / Pauline Reade
sixteen years old / vanished on her way to a disco / July

12 1963 / her body was found in 1987 / on Saddleworth Moor / John Kilbride / lured up on to the moor / sexually assaulted and murdered / by you two / you took a photograph / your lover Ian Brady posing on the edge of John's shallow grave / holding your pet dog / Keith Bennett / just twelve years old / body never discovered / he vanished June 16 1964 / Myra and Ian told nobody / this child's remains are hidden / so his family can never know / and lay their son to rest / Lesley Ann Downey / ten years old / murdered Boxing Day 1964 / the youngest victim / abducted from a fairground / taken to the house Myra shared with her grandmother / in Hattersley / and up in Myra's bedroom / Lesley was sexually abused / and tortured and / forced to pose for pornographic photographs / this ordeal was recorded on audio tape / by Myra and by Ian / by you Myra / that's you on the audio tape / it lasted sixteen minutes twenty-one seconds / for some reason I remember this one detail / the morning of your capture / you told the police / *no* / you said *we take Mothers Pride* / I remember that / cheap / white / bread.

Mrs Death and The Doctor

Nightingale Hospital, Marylebone, London

Mrs Death:
I'm feeling fine.
No, that's not strictly true . . .

Doctor Delano:
How are you feeling?

Mrs Death:
I've been feeling anxious . . .

Doctor Delano:
OK, do you want to explore this?

Mrs Death:
I want to . . . but I am worrying . . . I feel anxious.

This. It isn't normal and it isn't safe.

Doctor Delano:
OK, take a deep breath and exhale and inhale and that's it
. . . breathe . . . breathe . . . Now let's unpack this slowly.

Mrs Death:
Look, I don't know why I am here. I am normal. I mean
fine. The other doctor told me I am developing bipolar
disorder, but I just have mood swings. I think bipolar means
much more than just mood swings. I am not bipolar. My
mood swings are probably just exhaustion, a hormone imbalance, anxiety, low energy, low iron, I mean, no wonder I
have some depression, I admit I am Death and I am depressed
and exhausted . . . After all I have seen, it is insanity that
I am the sane and normal voice in here.

Doctor Delano:
You sound agitated today. Please remember, we try not to
use the term normal in these sessions. I mean, what is
normal? I am not normal, you are not normal, nobody is
normal, not really, and as for safe, well, what harm can come
from talking? Talk to me. Can you tell me more about Mrs
Death, can you talk about these voices . . .

Mrs Death:
It's not voices, Doctor, it's real, real, real conversations, real
and vivid conversations, enlightening conversations, inspira-

tional and lengthy conversations, poems, stories, songs, connections. I really haven't talked to anyone like this ever before.

Doctor Delano:
Of course. Conversations. OK. So tell me about these conversations you've been having? Who are you talking to, are you able to ask questions?

Mrs Death:
I have made friends with a human called Wolf. I've crossed a line . . . I speak with a mortal. Am I able to ask questions? Yes. I can ask Wolf anything, I don't always get a straight answer but I can ask anything and . . .

Doctor Delano:
And . . . go on . . . How do these conversations make you feel? Does Wolf respond? How does Wolf respond?

Mrs Death:
Wolf listens. I know it sounds strange, I know it does, but I . . . I don't know . . .

I don't know where to begin . . .

Doctor Delano:
Begin at the beginning. Take a deep breath. When did this start?

Mrs Death:
At the beginning? Seriously?

Doctor Delano:
Yes, start at the beginning, the very beginning.

Mrs Death:
Well, you should know . . .

Doctor Delano:
Take your time and tell me your version of events, tell me how this began . . .

Mrs Death:
From the beginning . . .

For thousands of years I listened. A huge part of the work of being Mrs Death is all the listening that I do. Since this world began, I have heard it all: I listen to the ending, I am there for their last words and last prayers. As they let go they tell me their life stories, regrets and fears and loves. My head is filled constantly with stories of great sacrifice and great stupidity, stories of great courage and great evil, stories of bravery and kindness, greed and fury, grief and tragedy, joy and love. I alone hear all of this and I process it and keep it locked inside me and I continue my work. I am Death. In a way I am just a glorified rubbish collector. I am a cleaner. I clean. I collect the spirits up and carry all those burdens away. And lately I've been feeling like it is never-ending and all-consuming and all too much. I feel like we are spilling over. I'm exhausted. I've been feeling emotional. I know it's just life, or rather death, but I've been . . . crying?

Doctor Delano:
There is nothing wrong with crying and no such thing as just life. Life can be all those things: exhausting and emotional. You are allowed to feel that strain. You really are too hard on yourself. You put yourself under so much pressure. Can you give me any examples, is there something that triggers these thoughts, is there something making you cry?

Mrs Death:
The other day — just one example — the other day, there I am sweeping through a town in Syria and I find I am in floods of tears. I stop and stand there in the rubble and debris and I wonder why, why? What the fuck am I doing here again, so soon, again? Twice in one week? And that same day I am in America, in a school for yet another mass shooting, and I am there, roaring my eyes out, clearing through, collecting all these souls of terrified dead teenagers. Then I am out in the channel, off the coast of France, collecting the murdered souls of another sunk dinghy, a make-do refugee raft filled with desperate people escaping war but being left to drown on purpose. My work has been overwhelming. So much death and war and destruction, famine and murder.

And suicide is on the rise. And deaths caused by malnutrition, poverty and austerity, poor housing and poor healthcare. We thought things would change! I remember Time and Life, the sun and moon and all the universe, well, we all laughed and thought that the twenty-first century would be an easier century. The human has evolved at an alarming rate. Can you all just stop laying eggs for five fucking minutes? Stop consuming everything? Just stop it, stop it, Life, can Life give us all some rest? Can we hit the pause button and take a piss and have a cup of tea and a nap, please?

Humans have found ways to access world communication and share intelligence, they can send medicine and ideas and solutions, they can share art and beauty, they can communicate their resolutions and solutions all with the click of a button. Yet I am as busy now as I was in 1066. I am as busy as I was with Attila the Hun. There was once a time of language barriers and the unknown: the size of the planet was a mystery, it was tribal; the humans didn't know how small the earth was and how connected and similar the human condition. Human tribes fought for territories, for land grabs and gold and power. And now it is the same thing, but there is the internet and Google Translate. Why aren't they looking up the millions of words for peace and love and using this phenomenal intelligence to find cures and share solutions? I'm joking a little, and maybe I am not joking at all . . . It seems the more information and communication humans have, the more stupid they are, the more facts and tools they have, the more they get distrustful, spreading fake facts and lies and ignorance and fear until they become stupefied and closed off from their hearts. When did caring become so unfashionable?

Believe me, I love my job, don't get me wrong: Death is the greatest honour. I am here to work with you, I am there for rebirth and for the ritual of soul and spirit crossing into my realm of Death, but I am ploughing through a flood of untimely and unnecessary and sudden and violent deaths, genocide, natural disasters, all caused by greed and destruction. And that's just the human souls. Do you know how many miles and miles of ocean life are being killed by plastic and pollution every second? The ice caps are melting and sea levels are rising. The depleting ozone. The climate crisis. Flood and fire! I mean, I am Death but this isn't what I signed up for! I am not here for this . . .

I am not here to destroy myself. I am not going to support the death of Death.

And don't get me started on the idiot people accidentally dying by taking selfies. Do you know how many people die because of selfies? People are dying taking photos of their own faces and falling off the Great Wall of China or tripping over into the Grand Canyon. I am doing the work of a dozen women here . . . Sorry.

Doctor Delano:

Never apologise, I am here for this, thank you for sharing. So tell me, how does Wolf fit into all of this?

Mrs Death:

When I am with Wolf we explore and dream. Wolf sits at my desk and I tell my secrets. I have grown to trust Wolf. I have made a human friend. Wolf has been talking to me every day this winter. Wolf and me write together, we write stories and poems together. Wolf says, *Hey Mrs Death, how are you today, are you alright? Who died today, do you want to talk about it? Do you want to get these feelings down on paper?* Wolf says, *Hey Mrs Death, do you want to talk about your experiences? Shall we write about the cigarette industry? Or the arms trade? Or fracking? Or the pharmaceutical companies? Or the oil companies? Or the manufacturers of guns? Wanna have a chat about the real monsters, the toxic greed and big corporate industries that are killing us all?*

When I am writing with Wolf I feel seen and heard, actually listened to for once; for the first time ever I am not just an invisible cleaner, clearing the dead bodies. Wolf writes with me. We write about my memories and my dreams for the future and what my legacy will be, at least what I would like it to be. Wolf asks me, *Will there ever be a day when Mrs Death will rest?* I don't have an answer for that. Wolf asks, *What happens if the earth is annihilated, what happens when all is flood and fire?* I say, *It will be messy, I know that much and that little.*

Doctor Delano, all I know for sure is unless the humans change the way they are living, they cannot change the way they are dying.

Doctor Delano:
We can change the way we are dying if we change the way we are living.

You have so much on your plate. You really are taking everything on your shoulders here. It sounds like you have a lot to process. Losing people – loss – it's a big parcel to unwrap and comprehend. I think the best possible way to deal with loss and trauma would be to write about it. This writing, it sounds very healthy to me. Use your creativity to process it. Grief is a big job. It is a big job you do and a lot of work and it sounds to me like you have reached a pinnacle, or perhaps a turning point . . . Do you feel like that? Do you feel comfortable enough to tell me any more? When did this friendship with Wolf begin? What draws you two together: did you choose Wolf or did Wolf choose you?

Mrs Death:
We found each other on Christmas Eve. It began with The Desk. Wolf acquired my old desk from a junk shop and it started then, a couple of months ago. I use The Desk as a vessel, a conduit, to speak to Wolf. When Wolf sits at The Desk and listens we can communicate through the veil. All

my poems and songs, my private thoughts, seep through Wolf's hands and fingers and out onto the pages.

But we go back much further than that. I met Wolf as a child. There was a horrible fire. Wolf was only nine back then and Wolf's mother died that night. Wolf howled a note so loud and so sad and so pure that I never forgot it. I never forgot that kid, that curly-haired kid standing barefoot in the road in pyjamas, an angel in all that black smoke and chaos. Lots of people died in that fire, it was a catastrophe, cheap housing, no fire alarms or sprinklers. Of all deaths, I don't know why but I never forgot that night or Wolf.

Doctor Delano:
Earlier you talked about safety: may I ask, are you safe? Is Wolf safe with you? Are you safe with Wolf? Do you feel safe?

Mrs Death:
What do you mean by safe?

Doctor Delano:
I mean is Wolf safe? Is Wolf safe talking to Mrs Death? Is Mrs Death safe with Wolf?

Mrs Death:
Death isn't catching! Hahaha, that is what Wolf keeps saying, *death isn't catching.*

Well, I don't know, what harm can come from talking about death? That's what you said. Talking is healthy. Writing is cathartic. We're talking now, you and me, and you're alive and fine, aren't you? . . . I mean, you haven't dropped dead by talking to me, have you?

Doctor Delano:
That's true. Writing can be cathartic.

Would you be interested in going to a writing retreat? I have friends in Ireland, they have a place, a tower, it is a place where poets and artists like you can go to retreat and write, it would be perfect for you . . .

Mrs Death:
That sounds amazing. Thank you. It's good to talk to you today, Doctor . . .

Doctor Delano:
I'll give you a letter to send to them in Ireland. I think it would be perfect for you to have a break. Talking is healthy. Talking and listening, talking and listening, that is what we do here, we're here to listen. And writing seems to be helping you too.

Mrs Death:
I have never spoken about this with anyone before. I just want to say thank you. That sounds wonderful. Doctor

Delano, it is such a relief to talk. You used the word cathartic. It has been cathartic to write and to talk. We need to give ourselves space to grieve, to be open and vulnerable and to tell someone about the business of Death. Lately it's been horrendous, every day another trauma, another battle, another bomb, another catastrophe, another tragedy. Death has been working hard; I have been working hard. Thank you, I would love to go to Ireland to write.

Doctor Delano:
You're welcome. I'll write you a letter of recommendation. I can tell you have been working hard . . . You're doing some great work here.

Mrs Death:
Thank you.

Doctor Delano:
Please don't think me rude, but you've never been gender specific in any of our sessions before this. I've never imagined death as a person, let alone as a woman. Death is a woman, you say, you identify as a woman. How does that feel, how does she feel, how does that manifest?

Mrs Death:
You're not alone. Nobody sees me. The world sees death as male. This is how it has always been. The artists, the

writers, the poets and storytellers, they've all imagined me, they have fictionalised death, but always as a male energy. They will tell us stories of a woman causing death but not being death herself. When we think of the female role in death, we might picture Greek or Roman mythology, the Medusa, Atropos, the vengeful Goddess or the siren luring sailors to their death. There is a female guardian of hell in Viking tradition and Nordic folk stories. You will find Kali Ma, the female incarnation of Shiva, as the powerful Goddess of destruction. We find women here as Goddesses and powerful deities in Asian cultures and African cultures and Caribbean folk songs and stories too. In Islamic and Middle Eastern folklore we have powerful queens and Goddesses: often depicted as an outcast woman or a witch, a hag, she is often destructive or motivated by malice. She is a vengeful crone, a woman of 'hysteria'. And often she is childless or barren, as though having a child is the natural and only thing that makes a woman a sensible woman, a real woman. Often even when a Goddess is powerful, she is enslaved by a curse to a male figure, to a devil or Satan character.

Then there are horror movies, with repeated themes of enslavement and submission, the Devil's concubine, a female vampire or pagan witch. We see cinematic images of the Devil's whores, naked women possessed by evil. Mystical witches in a circle dancing naked in some woods by firelight in a bloody ritual. There are women of magick, white magic or black magic and Voodoo spell-makers, African witch doctors and Caribbean Obeah priestesses.

None of these are me. They are not DEATH – Mrs Death – they are not Death itself: they do not do my work.

In the media, in the newspapers, there are horror stories of evil women capable of taking life – for example the Moors murderer Myra Hindley. But we don't hear of many famous serial killer women or female repeat offenders who act alone. Most female serial killers we hear of appear to work in a team, a pair, a deadly couple that kill, have you noticed that?

Only three women have ever been given whole-life sentences in the UK: Rose West, Myra Hindley and most recently Joanne Dennahy. Joanne Dennahy was a thirty-year-old mother of two and a triple murderer. These were the Peterborough ditch murders. She pleaded guilty on all charges in 2013. She hunted and killed men as though for fun, and allegedly wanted to be famous for her crimes. She appeared to enjoy frightening people. She threatened to kill Rose West within minutes of arriving in the same jail and they had to move her to another prison. I digress, but it is fascinating, don't you think?

We are programmed to believe that the female is here for birth, that she is a she, she is mother, she is here to nurture a soul inside her body and to feed the infant at her breast. That the woman may house the new life and soul, and feed and care for a soul, but she may not be the power that takes a soul. I am here. Death is a woman. I am a woman. Surely by erasing me we have erased this power? By never portraying a woman as the representative of Death, the boss of Death, the figure of Death itself, one could debate that an important and fundamental disempowerment takes place. Perhaps this is what erasure looks like.

All over the planet women are portrayed as nurturers, life-givers, life-providers, nurse and mother and carer. Women are here to respond, nurture and feed us, but not to have the final say, not to pull the trigger, close the curtains and press the exit button. We are told that God is a man in the sky and that the Devil is a man down below. The Christian Church is ruled by a pope, who is a human man and judge and jury. And our policemen and our laws are made and amplified by men. Time is also a male; we have been told there is a Father Time. And then the time of our death and our mortality – the Grim Reaper – is also depicted by a male figure in a black hood with a scythe.

It is exhausting how much space men want and how much credit and control man wants to take for mankind. Male is the God and creator, male is in the centre of the story, male is the narrator, the source of the fire; male as the light, male as the night and the dark and the war and destruction. Man holds all the cards. Think of the Sun and the Moon, the sky and the sea, the water and the flame, the air and the earth, the yin and the yang, the birth and the death, which is female to you and which is male? Think of the colours of the rainbow, red and yellow and pink and blue and purple and orange and green, which colours are female and which are male? Think of each and every star in the galaxy and tell me which is male and female? These spirits and energies, the gender of the world and our universe, how ridiculous it all is to me. Is oxygen male? Is air a boy too?

I have come here to walk the earth as human. I choose to be disguised and camouflaged. I live in the faces of the most betrayed and ignored of all humans. I live in silence. I am the words trapped on the bitten tongue. I am more than a statistic. I am more than another hashtag. I live in the heart of the poor woman, the black woman, the elderly woman, the sick woman, the healer, the teacher, the priestess, the witch, the wife, the mother and the girl. I am Death and I am quick. I am a rabbit and I can vanish. I can be anything I want to be. I choose the unheard and unspoken. I live in the silent scream and I will be silent no more and I have so much work to do . . .

Wow . . . I've never said all that before. I trust you, Doctor Delano . . . I trust you . . .

Doctor Delano:

Thank you for trusting me. You're doing some great work here . . .

Mrs Death:

I feel like you believe me. I am real. I think you believe in me.

Doctor Delano:

I do believe in you . . . I do.

Yes. You are real, of course.

Mrs Death:

REALLY REALLY REAL

breathing am I breathing?

Doctor Delano:

Yes . . . really.

Mrs Death:

I mean, put it this way, people will read your notes on this page and erase you, they'll presume Doctor Delano is a man, just because I have used Doctor, Doctor, won't they, Doctor? They will read Doctor Delano on a page and assume you are a male doctor and that it's a man, a male doctor talking to Mrs Death here today. But you are real, a real woman, and a real female person who is a *doctor* doctor in a real hospital trying to help me . . .

Doctor, you are real, and I am real, and it is all really real, it is an erasure, isn't it, *breathing am I breathing wait I think I have forgotten to breathe* . . .

Doctor Delano:
Real. Yes. You look pale. Do you need a break? Do you need some water?

Mrs Death:
You are real though . . . I am real . . . this is real.

MRS DEATH IS REALLY REALLY REAL

but what if I stop breathing am I breathing? I sometimes forget to breathe . . .

Doctor Delano:
Yes, real. I am real. You are real. Here, have some water? Would you like to rest? Wolf?

Wolf? Wolf? Wolf?

Wolf:
I'M NOT BREATHING . . . I CANNOT BREATHE . . . I CANNOT . . .

Doctor Delano:

WOLF! WOLF?

WOLF? BREATHE!

WOLF, WOLF!

WOLF?

Wolf: First Snow

Nightingale Hospital, Marylebone, London

They tell me I have to rest. They found me a bed and gave me a pill to make me sleep. I woke up here. I do not know how long I have been sleeping or if I am still dreaming. Or if I am awake. Same as it ever was. I know I am in a hospital bed. I have a green blanket and stiff white sheets. I remember this, I have been here before, this itchy green blanket that smells sterile. I have a tube in my hand and a really dry mouth. Water? Is there water? My throat is raw and sore. My eyes are puffy and hot. So much crying has happened. Outside it is snowing. I wish I could eat snow. Ice cream. Snowy ice cream would be lovely and I would push my hot face into it. Snow falls, patting gently at the window.

I turn my head and find Mrs Death sitting in the green chair by my hospital bed. She is vivid. She is so colourful today, more beautiful than I have ever seen her before. Her afro hair is decorated with orange-yellow marigolds. She is smiling at me. She nods at me and winks and swigs from a silver flask. Today she is Nina Simone – a young Eunice Kathleen Waymon – her big beautiful soul, her bright smile, a powerful heart beats in the room with me here today. I hear her heart, it goes: *Dum-dum . . . dum-dum.*

She cocks her head and asks: *do you want me to leave you alone, Wolf?*

She is a young Nina, toothy, grinning at me from the corner of the room. And Nina begins to sing, *trouble in mind,* so slow and so easy and so soft. I am gazing over at her and Nina is shimmering and gold and magenta and orange and flickering and fizzing. She is watching the snow out of the window, the soft feathery snow, the pure notes, the gentle music. Snowfall. I float here crying, I am crying, something is dying, winter is dying, Mrs Death is dying, Wolf is dying. I must be dead, I am in heaven, I must be in heaven, Nina is singing to me. I manage to whisper: *please don't leave me, Mrs Death . . . you're my best friend,* as I fall asleep.

Mrs Death: We Could Be Heroes

Bowie died. Prince died. Leonard Cohen died.

And everyone that made you feel beautiful and young is going, one by one and there is nothing you can do about it. Everyone who knew you when you were beautiful and young will all fade away. One by one. Nobody will be around to remember the young you any more. And your heroes will disappear, they will stop being there and then you will hear that they died and then you will die a little bit too. You probably haven't seen them for years. Nor listened to their music nor read their books nor watched their movies. But there was a time you had their poster on your wall, a shrine in your heart, they were the soundtrack to the good times, your glory days. You might go to their funeral. You might go to a bash in the local pub in their honour. This is how it will go. Your heroes die one by one.

You find you begin to be more sentimental, nostalgic, you reminisce and live in the glorious colours of the past, weeping for your heroes, as the future grows more papery, and time burns easy as tissue. The older you get the better you were, and the better they were. Music is a time machine to before: *There's that song, remember that song?* Music takes you back. And the most ordinary objects have value: a hair clip in an old make-up bag will take you back twenty years, you didn't even wear it much, but once you did and there you are again. Photographs are precious. Look at me. Look at before. Look what we did. Look what we wore. Look how we are now. Look. Look. Flashback. Look. Look. Look. Your body aches sometimes. You need glasses. You have a round belly now. You forget the names of things. You aren't as quick. You drop the ball.

Bowie is dead. Prince died. Leonard Cohen died. George Michael died. Jock Scot died. Howard Marks died. Gil Scott-Heron. Aretha Franklin. Maya Angelou. Toni Morrison. Bill Withers. Little Richard. Carrie Fisher. Princess Leia. What is going on? Who else will we lose? And who will be next? This isn't a joke. Circle the wagons, please protect Tom Waits, Joni Mitchell, Bob Dylan, Neil Young, Dolly Parton, Keith Richards, Stevie Wonder . . . And you sit and stare into the internet at the cult of public grief, performative grief. Every day, another star falls, another someone who meant something special to someone, who meant something special to a whole group of someones.

Some deaths mean everything to everyone. You read the obituaries and how brave and admirable these heroes were. How beautiful she once was. He donated so much of his wealth to the needy. You knew they were good people. Just look at the kindness in their eyes! Look at this twentieth-century photograph. Look how twentieth century we all once were. We were all so twentieth century! And what a life. What a legend. Read the truth: how they were rejected, how they were once considered failures, thrown on the heap, how they fought to survive, how they overcame life's obstacles. Once they were nobody and then they were somebody. And then they were old hat and then they were dead. And then they were someone special for all of you to remember. Che Guevara, Malcolm X and Bob Marley worn on your t-shirts forever! They blazed a trail, they smashed the system, they changed the game. You wish we all had that much courage. You wish people would say all this to the living when they are here — show your appreciation to your living heroes now, nice and loud, so they can hear you. Celebrate the living! Why are you waiting to outpour your love only when people die?

I just hope new heroes are being born this year . . .

Your heroes are here! Your heroes are all already here, darling. I see your heroes, I follow them, I watch them, they keep going and never stop. Your heroes are never giving up on their dreams. I see heroes at the food bank, your heroes are at homeless shelters, they take food to people sleeping in doorways. Your heroes are itinerant and broke, with no funding or arts grants. Your heroes are in Calais and Dunkirk, they wait by the shores of Mediterranean seas and volunteer to help the capsized boats and refugees. Your heroes are on the borders. Your heroes are down in Soho donating and distributing food and blankets. Your heroes are working overtime in the crumbling NHS A&E departments, your heroes are your doctors and nurses, your teachers and volunteers, people taking phone calls at the Samaritans and talking people down from the edge.

Your heroes march for human rights and the future of the planet. Your heroes are millions of school children protesting for the climate strike. Your heroes write graffiti and poetry. Your heroes are everywhere, they walk among us. Your heroes are waking up every day, skint and underpaid and busking it, your heroes are making work, beautiful books and music and art that you cannot see or find or read as is drowned out by all the propaganda and noise and adverts and the fear-mongering and the performative cruelty of politicians.

It is your job, your only job, to seek out and support and nurture heroes, this is all your responsibility. We can all do our part in the chain, to help others to help others, to help the others who help the others who inspire and help the others. Find the others! You are losing your libraries, museums, galleries, independent bookshops, pubs and music venues, so the beautiful spaces where thinkers and writers and artists could meet and share work and gather and blossom and dream are being erased. The survival of the hero is up to you all now. It is important, now more than ever, to fight for all of this, to fight for your rights, for your freedoms, for your art, poetry and music. Because you all need to be heroes, to step up, to speak up, to support each other. It is all about kindness, and you need the doers and the creators. You must pay attention to the ones who listen and hear and do and can and will and share. And to the people of science and art, books and music, otherwise what is the actual point of all of this? What was the point? Why are you all here if not for that? You are here for love. To share the love.

When hate is rising, then love can only rise higher.

We stare deeply now into the charcoals of winter and watch the last flames lick the chimney. The fires leave the sky and dance into the everything. All the warmth and all the joy is boiled in a soup of memory, we stir the good stuff from the bottom of the pot and hold the ladle up, *drink*, we say, *look at all the good chunks of goodness, take in your share of good times, good music, good books, good food, good laughter, good people, be grateful for the good stuff, life and death*, we say, *drink*.

Mrs Death: Black Star

I found David sitting on the sea front
He was perfectly calm
It was the perfect day for it
It's time . . . I began to say
But he was already seated
It was as though it was his idea
Some people come as if it is their will
Elegant, measured
As though they know it is just a ride
David sat in my carriage of hawthorn
The morning sea in the distance
Shimmering silver
As blue as January
As the carriage jolted and rocked
He blew a kiss to the horizon
It was as if he knew it was his time
My horses galloped along the sand

And David sang about the hawthorn
The hawthorn isn't in blossom yet
The hawthorn isn't in bloom
It was as if he knew
He wouldn't see another spring
It was as if he knew
Living was all a dream
And not many people do.

Wolf: Purple Rain

PRINCE
opened his secret show with
PURPLE RAIN.
I wasn't expecting that
it knocked me for six
tears sprang to my eyes
as soon as he sang
I cried
I heard the words for
SIGN ☮ THE TIMES
and tears streamed
down my face
I don't know
what it is about
PRINCE
yes I do
it is

everything
about
PRINCE
my love for
PRINCE
is bigger
than ever
it hurts
it is hard
it is difficult
to hero-worship
we don't write
about love
and respect
for an artist
until they die
we don't tell people
what they mean to us
we don't say
I LOVE YOU
until it is too late
and they are dead
and then we write
RIP on social media
this is not a review.
this is not a poem.
this is not a letter.
I don't know what this is.

I guess this is a confession:
I love you
PRINCE.
I LOVE YOU
Even. More.
Now.

Wolf: Let the Worms Chew the Fat

Nightingale Hospital, Marylebone, London

The staff at the Nightingale tell me they need the bed. They discharge me and let me come home. I apologise for all the drama. I am stupid. I forget to breathe sometimes and panic. I told them, *I don't need to be in a hospital and I think it was just a bit of a panic attack*, I said, *sorry*. They tell me I must go home and rest. I am suffering from depression and exhaustion, an iron deficiency and anaemia. But then one doctor told me they think I'm developing bipolar disorder. I don't understand what that all means? I cried my eyes out when they said that. I think the doctor said that because I told them I feel like I am on a rollercoaster. I have been very high or very low and very manic. I sometimes have blackouts and dizzy spells and coloured spots and shortness of breath. I forget to breathe sometimes. They asked me if I have been eating? I said I eat eggs. They asked me if I drink and I said yes, I drink wine. They asked me if I have been on impulsive spending sprees and manic episodes. I told them I impulsively bought an antique desk with my rent money. I watched as they typed that – *bought an antique desk* – and my heart sank as I felt some of the magic of The Desk shrink and slip away. They have put me on an eighteen-month waiting list and they said I have to return for more assessment. I have to take pills that I believe will numb me. Corks for my bottles of feelings. Dream plugs. I don't want them. I don't want to be a zombie and take these pills that might close the doorway to my visions. I won't take pills that might make my dreams disappear and my thinking neat as shopping lists.

I had to fill in a form:

On a scale of one to ten *are you depressed?*
On a scale of one to ten *are you restless?*
On a scale of one to ten *are you a danger to yourself or others?*

And I had to play along and promise, *No, I promise I am not a danger to myself and others.* I smiled and nodded like I understood it is protocol and they have to ask you these things before they send you home. And I smiled and nodded. *Yes.* I am suggestible because now I don't know if I am a danger to myself or not? I just kept nodding. I said that I fully intend to come back in eighteen months' time. I smiled and nodded all through it. I smiled and nodded and smiled and nodded. But inside I was screaming. On a scale of one to ten *are you silently screaming?* Then they gave me a mental health pack with leaflets with helpline numbers on it for suicide prevention. I also have a copy of a letter from Doctor Delano with details of a place in Ireland where poets can go to write. She told me it is a writers' sanctuary in a village called Cushendall in County Antrim. Doctor Delano has written this very kind letter of recommendation for me. It is worth a try, I suppose. I cross my fingers and hope that I can go there one day.

Outside and walking I go: left leg, right leg, one foot in front of the other.

On a scale of one to ten I feel exhausted. My legs are leaden, I ache all over. On a scale of one to ten I feel alone but mostly very relieved to be back outside and breathing real air and shivering. The sound of my own feet in my own boots on the icy snow. Crunch crunch crunch. The wind is icy, the pavement slippery. I pull on my black beanie hat which is stuffed in the pocket of my coat. I pull my hood up. Double protection. I look up to see white snowy plastic bags strewn in bare-branch trees under a grey shitty sky, and a one-legged pigeon picking at a discarded chicken burger by a frozen dog shit in a pissy bus stop – and it is familiar and it is London and I am glad of it.

I walk from Marylebone towards the bus stop near Baker Street station, dirty snow, city snow, black slush in the gutters. I have had such a weird heavy time lately. I think my hormones are out of control. I have been hypersensitive and hyperemotional. I have been having dark unwanted thoughts. I'm in an emotional washing machine. How do I navigate this? How do I stop this escalating? How do I cope? This session at the hospital felt like being fourteen again, puberty, riding a plane wreck through turbulence and the bad weather all my own self-sabotage and my own stupid fault. I kinda got sucked in by the doctors. I should have kept The Desk secret. I feel like I have grassed myself up and Mrs Death too. I was chewed up and spat back out by my own self.

I will be OK now, now I am free and on the outside. I like my own company best, I always did.

The only thing that scares me is this has reminded me that I do not get the same diagnosis every visit. I cannot get a straight answer from anyone about anything. All I know is this: I had a panic attack in my therapy session. I forgot to breathe. They made me stay in a bed and they gave me funny pills that made me have massive zombie sleeps, and now it is silent and lonely and I cannot find Mrs Death. I cannot hear her any more. The silence is deafening.

And isn't this what they do? They make you think you are the mad one? I think the doctors are mad. I think dentists are mad. I think the butcher, the baker and the candle-stick-maker are all mad. I think people are all mad, the way people all over the world are getting up and going to work every day in a job they all hate; it is all mad. I think eating chlorinated chicken is mad. I think not kicking up a fuss is mad. I think walking past homeless people like that couldn't be you one day is mad. I think the world is mad, mad, mad.

But what if this passion and fury and all this writing were always just the ramblings of an imbalanced mind? What if everything I ever wrote and created was just my mania talking? What is real and what are just feelings? And which are real feelings or just hormones or chemicals in your body? And pain and anguish, anxiety and grief, joy and jubilance, are these just imagined? And are you not really real and genuine in these emotions? And more pressing and to the point, what if Mrs Death isn't real? And what if all this time I was not a passionate person at all, but these experiences and feelings and poems have been nothing but the rants of a mental health issue? *Hey, there is nothing wrong with that,* you say, but we all know there is a stigma attached to it.

What if I made Mrs Death up? Is Mrs Death real? Where are you when I need you, Mrs Death?

I jump on the bus heading eastbound. It is dead quiet and empty upstairs. I sit down and lean to let my forehead touch the glass and I watch the city from above. The window pane is cool. There is frost and snow on the dome of the roof of Madame Tussaud's and I exhale slowly and empty my lungs and my breath fogs up the window and then I suddenly cry. And once they start, the tears won't stop. Hot tears on my cold cheeks and the cool glass. There is a hurt and a pain in my chest. I feel broken. I don't know what time or day it is. I don't know where I am. I am guessing it is time for me to go mental in Doolally town. The doctor has arranged to send me for further evaluation. She thinks I'm developing bipolar. I looked it up and I found out that bipolar and hormone imbalance and PMT and menopause and being an empath and being a human who gives a flying shit all share similar symptoms – mood swings, hypersensitivity, restlessness, insomnia, extreme highs and extreme lows, suicidal thoughts, restlessness, catastrophising and crying alone on buses. The world is in chaos, the earth is in climate emergency. There has been another shooting, this time a racist white supremacist Islamophobe burst into a mosque all guns blazing. We should all be crying on buses. What is wrong with everyone? I am not catastrophising. This is a fucking catastrophe. That doctor thinks I might be bipolar and every time I think about that word bipolar I start crying again. Look at me, that's me, Biracial, Bisexual, Bigender and Bipolar. That's my labels and my boxes, that's me, I'm the one you can see all alone crying upstairs on the bus. I am crying because I am afraid. I'm crying because this is probably the saddest and loneliest bus ride ever. I'm crying because maybe I am a bit mad. And maybe I am crying because you aren't crying with me right now, because you just aren't mad enough.

I close my eyes and listen. Nothing but the bus engine. Nothing but the wheels of the bus in the icy slush. Nothing but the city buzz. Nothing. Where is she? Where are you, Mrs Death? I cannot hear you any more. I am worried that the doctors dulled my senses and severed our connection. Sing to me. I am so alone without you. I no longer know of my life before you, before these real dreams. I long to sleep, and to stay asleep so that I am always with you. I don't know what that means. I don't know anything any more. If I try and die tonight, will Mrs Death be there? Will she come? If Mrs Death is there, I think I will be alright. If I try and sit with The Desk and die a little tonight, maybe she will come back and talk to me and remind me to live and save me? When we die, do we still think inside our heads? Can we talk to Mrs Death or does it go black and silent? Lights out. Close curtains. Shut down. Pennies on your eyes. A penny for your thoughts. And all is still. And will the approach of death be a numbness? Is death all feeling going? The feeling is going, the air is leaving us, emptying, we are like a deflating balloon. All lost into the wind and gone. Nothing but the flabby shell of who you once were remains. You are a fleshy carcass rotting away. Your bones, your teeth, all mulched into the earth. The soul departed. The heart stopped. The urgency over. No more rush. The silent song. No hunger. No noise. No rapture. Just gone. Lifeless. An empty bag of bone marrow and calcium and rotting proteins. We are nothing and nowhere.

Or do we sprout new shoots like potatoes? I hope so. I would very much like to be a potato. I would be a good potato. I like new potatoes and fresh mint. I like chips. I like mash. I like baked potatoes with beans. Yes. That sounds good. I would like to be pushed under the mud, to sprout new shoots and make new potatoes. New new potatoes.

Or will my soul soar? Will I fly and leave my body behind? Will I leave my body a bit like an overcoat, hang my flesh on a coat hook, kick off my bone skeleton shoes and watch my soul go, let go, and get up and dance with Mrs Death?

Or is it more like the curtain on a plane between economy and first class: they close the curtain for the journey, so you cannot see all the good stuff the posh folks can eat on the other side. On the other side of the curtain there are the dead souls in better seats with nicer meals and free drinks. The VIP red-rope barrier: if your name's not down, you're not coming in. The golden ticket to death. The vast divide. Those on the edge, separated by a curtain, the outside and the inside, the living and the dead. Is there ever a blurring of the lines? Is that what this is, am I half dead? Half alive? Am I both Martha and Marsha?

The bus stops at King's Cross station and an old lady boards. She has bags and bags of empty plastic water bottles. Hundreds of plastic water bottles, enough to build a raft. She takes ages to climb the stairs of the bus, clumsy and heavy-footed, and she sits at the very front. I stare at the back of her matted dreadlocked hair and woolly hat. I can smell her – it is a bad smell of stale beer and drains and rain and urine. She wears many layers and many colours, threadbare and filthy, several coats and scarves. She has ripped plastic bags tied onto her feet. Slowly she turns to smile at me. I know her smile. I smile with relief. I know her, that broken soul and those sad and yellow eyes. She smiles and I see she has no teeth. It is she. She is here with me. She hums a tune.

Oh, where do we go when we die, Mrs Death? Where will I go when I die? Will you come and see me there? Will they lay me down in a box and bury me under the ground? Mrs Death is here with me again. I close my eyes to listen.

She closes her eyes and sings: *Just let me lay down, where the dead lay, in the summer, in the morning, let me lay down, where the dead lay, in the summer, in the morning.*

Mrs Death, sing to me, sing.

Mrs Death: The Remembrance

Let me lay down where the dead lay
In the summer in the morning
Let me lay down where the stones are cool and grey
Let me lay down where the dead lay
In the summer in the mourning
Where the dead sleep may I lay my head
And what are they dreaming inside the cold earth
And what are they thinking we think of them now
Let me lay down where the dead lay
In the summer in the morning
Let me curl up in the graveyard to sleep
And what were they dreaming
And what were they hoping
And what were they wishing for us all today
And would they be proud of the messes we're making
And would they still die for us now
Oh I'm so tired, so tired

Of fighting and wishing and
Hoping we'll be something more
So let me lay down, let me lay down
Where the dead lay their head
Let me lay down, lay down
Let me lay down my troubled head
And would they be proud
Of the messes we're making
And would they still fight and die for us now
Let me lay down where the dead lay
In the summer in the morning
In the mourning

Wolf: My Grandmother Rose Willeford

Wolf dreams a childhood memory

Wolf has an empty jam jar. Wolf looks up at Grandmother Rose and Wolf asks, *What are the three most important things in life?* Grandmother Rose is peeling potatoes at the time, standing at the sink. It is about to rain and the washing is on the line. Rose wonders if she should fetch it in or wait and chance it. The potatoes are muddy and old, the skins as thick as shoe tongues. It has been a long life for the potatoes, for the rain and for Grandmother Rose too. She sighs and feels tired, very tired of her curious grandchild's questions, tired of the house, tired of her shape and the shape she must be to fit in this world. She is so tired. She is tired of the curve of her back and the curve of the earth.

Her grandchild Wolf grows impatient and yanks on Rose's apron and Wolf asks again: *What are the three most important things in life?* Grandmother Rose shakes her head slowly, noticing her hands are cold and numb in the dirty potato water. One raindrop spits onto the kitchen window, followed by five more, *spit spit spit* says the old rain, *spit spit*. The washing will get wet unless Rose is quick, the sky is a dark violet colour.

Hey, Wolf tries, one more time, *what are the three most important things in life?* The potatoes are peeled and bald in a bowl of salt water. Rose wipes her hands and darts out of the kitchen door to gather the washing from the line. The rain falls sudden, in sloops, rainwater runs and slurps from the gutter; the clean sheets are soaked through.

Wolf stands by the door for a time, watching the rain batter the laundry, old Rose standing in the old roses growing in the garden. Wolf takes it all in: the apple tree, the long green grass, the purplish sky. Mrs Rose Willeford all white-haired. The white bedsheets, her mouth full of clothes pegs, her apron pocket bulging with more wooden clothes pegs. Wet apples, wet grass and the wet old lady. Wolf leaves the empty jam jar on the step to fill with raindrops.

Old Man Willeford: The Tiger

You think you know someone. I mean, *know* someone, like your mother, like your daughter, like your own wife. You think you know someone like the back of your hand, and then slap, they go and die and leave you and you are left with all their things and you have to ask yourself: *Who was she?* You look at their things and you have to wonder.

The funeral was nice and quiet. Everybody said the funeral was special, it was a special day for a special lady. Everyone on their best behaviour. No drama, I mean, nice and respectful. After the service we came back to the house. Not too much to drink. There was too much food though, cousins came bearing glass dishes of brown stew and rice and coleslaw, enough coleslaw to . . . something or other, enough coleslaw to feed an army, I don't know, I am losing my train of thought.

Where was I? I am trying to think about this: you think you know someone, like really know someone, like your own wife, you think you know your own wife. Rose and I, we got married young, we married when she was seventeen and I was nineteen. That's a long time to live with someone. I'm not saying our marriage was perfect. We stayed together, richer or poorer, in sickness and health, and all that but . . . You think you know someone, that's all I'm saying. You think you know someone, and then they just die and leave you. They go and they ain't coming back. And you're left with things and clothes and bits and pieces, their bills and bank statements, pieces of paper, boxes of letters and birthday cards, pictures of the Royal Wedding of Prince Charles and Lady Diana Spencer, and a white china rabbit, and that is when you find out, it is then when they are gone that the person is different to what you always thought . . . is all I'm thinking . . . You think you know them, but maybe you never knew them at all.

Maybe we never know each other really. You marry a girl and she's a sweet, sweet girl, a good, good girl. I mean her father was the village preacher back home. She went home back to Jamaica and doted on her family, had nothing but a kind heart and a good word for everyone. But then what do you know, she's a tiger. Wild tiger. Hungry. Beautiful. Why she never said? In sixty years of marriage not once, not one clue. I married a tiger. Me? I was married to a tiger all these years.

And next thing I know I am sitting there with my head in my hands, looking at photographs of this tiger and thinking, *Wow, I never saw her like that.* This person I was married to was a tiger all along. And then, oh boy, then you really know what's what. There you are, a grown man, a foolish old man, crying alone. All the tears skidding down your face and crashing into your white beard. You weep alone all day. All morning and all afternoon. All alone. Drink something. All alone. It is dark when you stop sobbing. *You stupid man,* you say, *you a fool. You were married to a tiger. And all you saw was a reflection of yourself. You stupid, stupid man.*

You stare into an old photograph. It is 1962, Hong Kong. Your wife. Look at her. Look at her. Look at her. Rose. She was a wild cat, she was a tiger. A real tiger. All I saw was a wife. A cook. A cleaner. A mother. She was trying to show you she was a tiger all along . . . Look!

Look at those eyes, that face, and look at those claws. I feel you now, Rose.

I feel it now alright.

Your sharp claws.

I feel them now.

Mrs Death: The Death Card

Only she that is invisible can do the work of Death. And there is no person more silenced than the woman, talked over, walked over and ignored than the woman, the poor woman, the poor old woman, the poor old black woman, your servant bent over a mop, cleaning the floor of a hospital.

Did you see me today? Did you walk past?

Today I bleach and sanitise toilets. I wash floors and mop up your waste and spillages, I am cleaning up your shit and your vomit. I like hospitals and surgeries, the conversations I overhear in hospital canteens and waiting rooms. Places where people come and go. I sit and watch you come and go, you say, goodbye and hello, come and go, goodbye and hello. It's as though you are not connected to each other. Goodbye, you say, be brave, you say, clinging on to that one last squeeze of the hand. You give a funny little wave as they wheel you into the operating theatre. You don't have to touch to touch, to see to feel each other. You were designed to be in contact without contact, to communicate without phones, to call each other to each other's minds. Humans still have so much to learn. But in times of difficulty, when you are in pain and trauma, accidents and emergencies, you draw breath together, you connect, you're most tuned in and alive and alert. When you're sitting in a hospital waiting room, you're aware of clocks and space and time, separation and reunion, your chance and your fate. Humans were built to care for each other, to share, and to nurture, just like the nurturing survival instincts of the mother polar bear, the emperor penguin or the matriarch elephant. The history and the biology of humanity, your inheritance of medicine and science, it is phenomenal.

Laura and Michael sit holding hands in the hospital waiting room. Laura bites the fingernails of the other hand. They have been pensive, waiting for over three hours and still no news. Nothing but waiting. There is nothing longer than waiting when you know you are waiting for some waiting to stop.

Do you want another tea? Michael asks and Laura shakes her head *no* and sighs heavily.

He bows his head in his hand. His eyes are red, his face pale from shock. Laura pats his shoulder and tells him again that it was just an accident. *Don't worry*, she keeps saying, *kids bounce, kids are much more sturdy than they look.* Why is she making him feel better? Honestly? She is furious with him, underneath, but now is not the time to berate him for his drinking. And Michael cannot process it, he cannot hear Laura's words of comfort. All he hears in his head is the smashing of glass and impact. His mind plays it over and over, the tinny song of an ice cream van, the sun in his eyes and reaching for his shades. Then the bang, the collision, the dull thud on the bonnet. His shattered windscreen, the glass and the blood and the horror and the screams. It was all his fault. Idiot. His eyes start to blur again, filling with hot wet tears. He could have killed Julia. What if he has, what if he has killed her? Was he driving too fast? Will she be OK? Oh dear God, let her be OK . . . *I'm so sorry*, he says again, *I am so sorry, Laura, what have I done? I am so sorry.* Michael gets up and begins pacing again. Laura is staring at the floor and chewing on the skin on the side of her thumb.

I am here. I am watching. I am in the busy hospital waiting room. Mrs Death is listening and mopping the floor. I know the child has a broken arm, a nasty cut to the head and some bruises. But she will live, she will be OK, her name is Julia and she will have a scar for life. I am not here for Julia today. This will be one of those 'nearly died' stories because she will live.

And I know one day when Julia grows up she will point at the scar and yell, *Tequila!*

She demands this shot in a beach bar in Thailand. *I deserve a free shot*, she is saying, *I nearly died, I nearly died when I was nine.* The barman is giving free shots for near-death stories, it is a drinking game, and the barman smiles and pours the shot of tequila and Julia will knock it back and tell her tale. *I really nearly died when I was knocked over chasing an ice cream van, look at my scar!* She will lift her fringe and point, *Look. My own dad ran me over! My father was drunk, he shouldn't have been driving, stupid idiot, the car hit me and I flew through the air, hit the bonnet and went right over the roof, I could've died, but I only broke my arm! SHOT!* she'll call out and they'll do shots and share near-death experiences under the full moon. The warm sand beneath their toes, damp bikinis and t-shirts, one German and one Italian and two Aussies and an English girl doing shots, and it will be the best of best times, they will be friends forever they say and it is the funniest drinking game in the best beach bar in Phuket.

Several years on from this holiday, Julia is found naked and dead in a hotel room in Saigon. She rents a room in Ho Chi Minh City and trades as a fortune teller in the nearby streets. Police are called to the hotel in the city's backpacker district. The staff break into her room and find her body in the initial stages of decomposition. Some have rumoured that she gave a powerful Thai gangster an incorrect and unfavourable tarot card reading. Her Death card is the Tower card.

Mrs Death is here, I am here, but not for Julia, not today. Julia sleeps like a fairytale princess and she will wake up soon enough. It is so tempting to tell Laura and Michael not to worry, but that is not how this works. Nor how I work. I could tell Laura and Michael to dissuade their daughter Julia from being drawn to the dark, not to go to Thailand, not to get involved with Thai gangsters or under-estimate the power of tarot. Instead I tell them to breathe together. They breathe and pull closer, Laura and Michael, they've been going through a rough patch, this is an oppor-tunity for them to see each other differently, to remember what's important. They will be OK.

I leave them.

I squeeze the mop in the bucket and wheel it all down the echoing hospital hallway. It is time to pay a visit to Old Man Willeford in intensive care. My dear Wolf, your grandfather Old Man Willeford just had his second heart attack . . .

Mrs Death won't miss death, not this time.

Wolf: Now You Are Gone

The funeral of Old Man Willeford

I can write about you
I have so much to say
none of it is nice
your hard hands
your whisky breath
dead now all dead
it is not much colder today
than when you were alive
your name will never be mentioned
without a sad shaking of the head
that is what you leave me with
a sad shaking of the head
today I must attend your funeral
I walk around a supermarket
looking for items to fill this feeling

I struggle to choose flowers
plump white roses too lush
lilies too sweet
iris too bruise-purple
I buy sherry
I swig sherry in the car park
I know I'm not normal
but normal people
drink sherry
at funerals.

Mrs Death: Raven

The funeral of Old Man Willeford

What if I told you
Your funeral will be at half past three
On a cold Monday in winter
Frank Sinatra warbles
Through scratchy speakers
I arrive early and wait outside
Ravens gather in a bony tree above
As your hearse pulls in
Looking away, looking up
I count ten, then a dozen or more
Black bird shapes in black branches
Crude paper cut
Shadow puppets
Against the lead sky
Making such a fuss

Swooping, anxious, late
Screaming *kraa kraa kraa*
Flocking unkindness
I count fifteen and then
Twenty and then more
A conspiracy of ravens
In the tree above you

What if I told you all this
As the pallbearers
Open the door of the hearse
The light changes and sours
And you will be there and there you are
In a coffin the size of a feeling
they haven't organised yet
He is in that box
I whisper
There you are
A wreath of red, white and blue
Queen and country and the RAF
Your coffin the weight of everything unsaid
Your dirty secrets and filthy lies
And just as I think that
Two ravens fight and
Descend like Spitfires engaged in battle
They tumble and tear through the sky
Snapping a whole tree branch
Black wing and skirmish

Crashing war planes and
Broken feathers and
A chorus of *caw caw*
A scream from the unkindness above
Beaks jab, a ferocious fight on the lawn
The birds like two brawling blood-drunk fools
It's a knife fight in a Hong Kong alleyway
It's a slap for your wife
It's your daughter flying through a pane of glass
It's being too afraid to be alone in a room with you
It's the belt buckle end of a whipping
The birds peck at black shiny eyes
The unkindness cheering in the tree above as
One raven pins the other down
By the wing, by the throat

What if I told you about this moment
The violence of ravens
The broken tree, the miserable sky
Your funeral, your coffin
And all it stands for
Because of the way it has always been
The dark it always was with you
Always this feeling
The black beak and sharp claw
A screech of unkindness
White noise cruelty
This bleak bitter Monday in winter

The lifeless black trees
The wounded raven
The horrible truth
They watch them lift and carry you
And follow your coffin in
And watch you burn
Once and for all.

Mrs Death Watches TV

Wolf at home in the small attic room above the Forest Tavern pub, present day

Mrs Death sits with me. We drink red wine and flick through TV channels. The cacophony of phony canned laughter, colour and noise and singing and dancing and shouting competitions, celebrity shine, reality show time of a Saturday night family entertainment.

She pauses on a sixties crooner, he is singing the song everyone knows and afterwards everyone claps. The young TV host coos and preens and calls him a national treasure. The raucous live studio audience all cheer and applaud and online #nationaltreasure is trending.

The old crooner is orange and oily he says *thank you* and blows a kiss and waves to the camera. He takes a bow. Fake tan, fake charm, beaming his fake white teeth with a confident grin.

For tonight his sexism, his racism and elitism is all brushed over, his penchant for child pornography and his connections with Members of Parliament, lords and oligarchs and filthy tycoons are not mentioned. It is neatly swept aside and disguised by his Christian God-talk, his public charity work, his knighthood and his multimillions in the bank. Nothing can touch him.

Or so he thinks. Mrs Death chuckles and raises her glass to the screen, *I'll see you soon enough*. Mrs Death downs her wine in one, takes a long draw on her cigar.

She says, *His name is on my list, and when he meets me it ain't gonna be pretty*.

Mrs Death: The German Hitchhiker

County Antrim, Northern Ireland, April 1988

Except she wasn't a hitchhiker. She didn't take risks and get into cars with strangers. She was a German backpacker from Munich, exploring the UK and Ireland on an inter-rail ticket. She was aged eighteen and travelling alone. She was blonde and good-looking. She was staying in youth hostels. She did not have any accommodation booked for Ireland, and she was running low on money; we know this from her last diary entry.

What else do we know? We know she boarded a ferry from Scotland to Ireland that would have landed in Larne as it was getting late. She was alone and visiting Ireland as a tourist during the Troubles. Northern Ireland was a dangerous place then. And this unsolved case stands out because this is such an unusual, brutal case.

This is one of Northern Ireland's highest-profile unsolved murders, with one of the largest DNA screenings ever undertaken, comprising more than 2,000 samples. Police went door-to-door taking swabs and collecting DNA of hundreds of men, which was unprecedented for the 1980s when DNA screening was new.

She was seen boarding the Stranraer to Larne ferry. However, no witnesses saw her disembark. Did she break her rule and get in a car and catch a lift from a stranger she met on the ferry? Perhaps.

Her body was found two weeks later on April 20th on the floor of Ballypatrick forest. She had been beaten and sexually assaulted, she'd suffered head injuries, her face was bruised and she had a broken neck.

Isn't it so strange that the murderer or murderers did not bury her? People say they did not try to hide nor conceal her body. They didn't weigh her down and drown her in the nearby lake or throw her off the jagged rocks into the Irish Sea crashing below. People say they left her face-down in the middle of the forest path. Her bags and backpack, her belongings all strewn around her. Why did they leave her on the forest floor exposed like that? Did they have a farmhouse or basement somewhere to keep her prisoner for two weeks? Was she held captive before her body was dumped in the forest?

They say she gave a good fight. Her fingernails were caked with blood and skin. One man was questioned in Ballymoney with scratches on his face. Someone knows something, someone hid someone. Somewhere somebody cleaned this up that damp April night in 1988. Some have said they saw a girl fitting that description around the Cushendall and Cushendun camping areas. Others say that she probably took a lift with a lorry driver and he drove her into the forest and then attacked her.

In spring 2018 the police issue a statement that they are *tantalisingly close* to solving the case. They arrest two men aged sixty-one and fifty-eight in the Loughguile area. They are released without charge. The police believe that the perpetrators knew the forest in detail, they believe someone is covering for someone. Loyalties shift and Time changes things. Her dead body was found deep into the vast forest, an area not used by the general public. The local people of the rural surrounding villages – Cloughmills, Loughguile and Armoy – refuse to believe that it could be a local man. The word down the pub is that it must have been military, an English soldier or soldiers, driven crazy with bloodlust from all the Troubles and all the killing that was happening around them then. The military have their own law. So the soldiers that were stationed there then, were they tested and swabbed too? And has their DNA been included in the screenings?

What happened next? Did she get in a strange car with soldiers? Was she taken somewhere else before the forest? Was she held captive? What were her stomach contents? Was she drugged? What happened to that poor girl?

They knew. When they came home so late they knew.
   When they came falling through the door they knew.
   They were dishevelled and they knew.

Their knuckles were bloody and filthy, mud caked the knees of their trousers and the soles of their shoes and they said nothing. Their face was scratched, they knew. They said nothing. It has been thirty years now. They worry and sweat in the night. They twist and turn in the sheets. They live with it now, they won't stay in the old house, not now, and not since then. They sweat in the night, they twist and turn in the guilt, they do not rest, sleep is no friend to the guilty. They read the papers, they know the police are closing in. And thirty years is a long time to sweat. Thirty years is long enough to not sleep for worrying about a thing. Thirty years is too long to bite your tongue.

She wasn't just a hitchhiker, say her name, her name was Inga Maria Hauser.

Everything Is Nothing But Nothing Is Worth Something to Someone

Now they are gone. There used to be a grandmother and a grandfather living in this house but they are not here any more. This was the house of Old Man Willeford and his wife Rose. I lived here for five years, from aged nine, but then I ran away. That is all over and they are all gone now. When someone has been a bad person, or a cruel person, the grieving is strange. This is the end of a house and home. Nothing and everything, everyone and no one. Everything is nothing, nothing lasts, nothing is finished and nothing is perfect.

I did not want to live with my mother's father and mother. I was there in my pyjamas, the fire and madness, my bare feet, the tip of my tongue in the gap where I lost my tooth, and then suddenly I was here living under this roof and sleeping in that box room. My mother would not have given me to these people. She had nothing good to say about her own childhood: she physically shrank and shook her head when Old Man Willeford was mentioned. She also shrugged and shook her head sadly about Rose. When my mother was alive we never visited her parents. There was no apple-pie love here. No jolly family Christmas, no Easter egg hunts, no learning to swim or being taught to ride a bicycle, no happy childhood memories, not one, not with them, no, there was no blowing out the candles on the birthday cake. I was nine, turning ten, and it was as good as going to live with strangers. But on paper they were family and my next-of-kin and so my fate was sealed. After the fire, after the first day I met Mrs Death, they were given custody and off I was sent. That first night sleeping here, up in that tiny box room, was the longest of nights, a long darkness, a cold hole, that lasted five years until I ran away . . . and now they are all dead and here I am.

I enter through the front door. This is the very door I slammed aged fifteen and ran from, this is me, I am crossing the threshold, a doorstep I swore I would never darken again. Mrs Death has been here, I can smell her. I step over several months of unopened post cluttering the step. The hallway smells of musk and damp. Acrid wafts from the downstairs toilet, bleach and urine. Sickness happened here. Neglect. Sorrow. Grief. I'm at the house where death happened, where Mrs Death has been at work. Mrs Death took my grand-mother swiftly but Old Man Willeford, she took her time, she pushed him, now, didn't she?

I touch the garish orange wallpaper and through my finger-tips the rooms echo with all the years. I can feel it and hear the orchestra of the past and the once-living. The hollow song of ages, the chorus of time passing, the faint sound of a ticking clock, laughter, tears, boredom, anger, fear. Mostly fear. This was a house that was filled with worry and fear; this was a house of tears. A place where things were thrown. I hear a slap and cry, a broken glass, the smashed plates, followed by long and stilted silences. Unhappy drinking happened here, my grandfather's hard hand clutching the bottle, the jangle of ice in a tumbler of whisky. This was a house where you bit your tongue and held your breath. There it is below my shoes, the carpet of eggshells, trodden on, oh so very carefully. This is a house of secrets and all that hurt vibrates even now. I feel it all. This was an ordinary house on the outside and inside it was never a happy home.

On the hallway walls the remaining pictures hang askew. There is a sun-stain patch on the wall, it betrays where for decades was a gold-framed painting of tigers, not a great painting but a familiar shape even in its absence. Objects are meaningless, everything is nothing, but somehow everything is worth something to someone. Everybody must be worth something to somebody.

The people are all gone now. The wife, Mrs Willeford, Rose, my grandmother, if she were alive, she would be furious to see her home in a mess like this. If she were alive, she would be weeping. The curtains hang crooked. Everything is in the wrong room and wrong place. But we mustn't be precious about things. Things are just things, you cannot use things in your grave. I find it peculiar, the random objects people keep and the things we discard. It is so odd the stuff we hoard and the important items that get lost – we lose honesty and trust and love but hey here's a Blackpool Tower snow-dome paperweight; we make sure to keep that safe instead.

There are items you can see my grandmother Rose obviously meant to 'keep for best'. I find her paper umbrella from Hong Kong. It is ripped and has a snapped spoke, now how did that happen? It hung from that hook by the living-room window for all these years, decades, dusty and untouched. Other people are not careful with other people, I mean, with other people's precious things. Only the dead know why these things were kept and treasured.

Wrap your life in a tissue and save it for best.

Home is where the heart is and hearts got broke in this kitchen. I remember, I can feel it and I can hear it, the kitchen table remembers, the walls remember, the carpet remembers. I remember, I remember a cacophony of a Sunday dinner, the chatter, the talking, a chink of sunlight hitting the spot where the pot steams, a moment of happiness, togetherness . . .

Shush, the news, listen to the news, bloody politicians, shush, bloody listen,
you're not listening, bloody listen, you never listen! Wolf, how many times
I have to tell you? How many times? Bang! Listen! Bang! Listen! Bang!
Bang bang bang!

He always shouted. I don't like being shouted at. I don't like
being shouted at when I am eating. It is hard trying to chew
and not listen when you are being shouted at when you eat.
I don't like being shouted at in the bath. I don't like being
shouted at when I am naked. I don't like being shouted at
in bed. I don't like being shouted at when I have only just
woken up. I don't like being shouted at when I am trying to
read a book. I don't like being shouted at when I am looking
out at the rain. I don't like being shouted at because I forgot
something. I don't like being shouted at because I don't know
something. I don't like being shouted at because I am not a
real girl and because I am not a real boy and because I am
not a real person. Fuck. I am crying again.

I stand in the kitchen and take a deep breath, my mind
searches for recall, the smells, the spicy aroma of jerk chicken
and rice and pea. The sizzle of plantain. Curried goat. This
was the smell of this kitchen, tender succulent meats, chilli
and ginger and herb and spice. The sound of my grandmother sucking out the bone marrow, chewing on the
knuckles, grease around the mouth and fingers, slurping,
licking, feasting. How many around that round table that
one time? How did we all fit? Oh boy!

I remember how she smiled for one second, her smile was like a pale winter sun coming out from behind a cloud then swiftly returning to grey. But there had to be some glimmer of hope, occasional happy times, some reason she stayed with the old bastard all those years. There had to have been good times, so we would trust and open ourselves up . . . yes . . . only to be slapped back down again. Up and down we go.

Every good memory I have of this house is followed by a stink, the sinking feeling, the next event, a doomy feeling and a shadow. This house of cards fell with a clatter of shattered promises, dirty secrets and broken ties. The teapot handle is all her fingerprints. I reach out and hold the handle. I hold the chipped handle that was once held by her – by my mother's mother and the mother of the house. I can feel her, I can hear her now. I suppose she wasn't a bad woman; she was surviving, her marriage, her choice, her life. She loved her husband no matter what. She covered up for him.

Rose begged me not to go to the police. How the kettle boiled and the tea pot was filled over and over again by my grandmother, by his wife, by the woman of this house. Her glasses steaming up as she poured. *Oh boy. Put the kettle on. Oh boy. Put the kettle on. Oh boy. Put the kettle on.* It is like tea is everything, tea makes everything alright again.

She said quietly, *Do you want tea? Have some tea.* My eyes were hot, my heart punching through my chest. I looked her in the eyes as I pushed my tea cup off the edge, it splashed as the china cup smashed onto the linoleum. I was too angry to speak to her for another second. That is when I left. I slammed that front door and never returned . . . until today.

This ghost of a love, how it coughed and spluttered to burn; I can see her now, all ash and dust. This house is dead: it is nothing but the lonely song of a woman in a sad and lonely life. Trapped. My grandparents were prisoners of their own lies, a tangle of ropes of lives all knotted in deceit. No life is ever tidy, no journey easy and no path runs straight. And what we leave behind is so strange and incoherent.

In the sitting room I find a leather box. It is filled with newspapers from the day of the Royal Wedding, magazine cuttings and pictures of Princess Diana and Prince Charles. This is the hard evidence of a life, of an existence: diaries, photographs, records and books. An old RAF uniform. Some silver cufflinks. A white china rabbit. I put the china rabbit in my pocket.

Three nails jut out of the wall – remember, three wooden ducks flying up the staircase. All that is left is the sentimental, the memories attached and detached. Leather photo albums – turn up the volume on these images – the good times past, parties and birthdays, holidays, weddings and funerals, births and deaths. There were once some good times, see! Look at the big happy faces, the cousins, second cousins, all the same eyes, or is it same forehead, same nose? I remember this photograph being taken and how he said, *Why you can't sit still, Wolf? Hurry up and take the picture, sit still, for crying out loud, Wolf, will you sit still! Why you never still, child? Say cheese!* Capture the moment, *snap, snap, snap,* the moment when life was happening, and all of this was unimaginable, the time when you were all grinning and framed in the moment, in this time, this year, this place.

Objects are meaningless. No and yes.

Everything is nothing but somehow everything is worth something to someone, just as everyone is worth something to someone. I'm done. I leave through the back door. The garden is wildly overgrown. The old roses have grown chaotic and tall, their fat pink faces grin down at you. I remember these roses, they used to smell divine, but they are covered in greenfly now. My grandfather loved this garden and Rose loved roses but neither loved me.

I remember Old Man Willeford would stand by that kitchen window and suck his teeth and grumble about the weather, all weather, the frost, the rain, the sun, all the weather was against him and his garden. Before any thunderstorm he was like the sky, he rumbled and grumbled along with the stormy weather as though he was made of cloud. The pear and apple trees have grown tall and unkempt, all are heavy with new fruit. This year when that fruit ripens and hangs heavy on the branch there will be nobody here to make fruit pies, crumbles and chutney. This abundance will windfall and rot in the overgrown weeds.

We leave all this behind. Everybody goes in the end and leaves this: odd socks; a box of silver cutlery; letters that mean everything and nothing; newspaper articles of a fairy-tale wedding and photographs of before; an overgrown garden. All I take is this one item, a white china rabbit. Even I know there is no bargaining with Time – Mrs Death was called and she came. She took the wife first and swiftly. And Old Man Willeford, husband, father, grandfather, lover, abuser – Mrs Death took him last. He died alone, he died knowing what alone really is. There is alone and there is dying alone, that's as alone as you can be. I did not run to his bedside to hold his hand. I was told he was dying but I didn't go to the hospital. I have to live with that. He died knowing he was not forgiven by me. He did not get away with it. And this is the end of that, that man in that house, the end of the many secrets and lies, the violence and hurt. I can feel all of it vibrating in the walls, rumbling in the brick, which of course will be a problem for the new family who buy this place.

It is then I have the strangest thought: Mrs Death will leave me soon.

I pick some sage, leave it on the back doorstep.

There is a jam jar on the step. It is filled with three things: green scum water, a dead bee and unanswered questions. I pick it up and empty it onto the long yellow grass. The three most important things in the world do not fit into a jam jar, I know that now. I say the words *Love Love Love* into the jam jar. I hear it echo, hollow and true.

Wolf: The Tower

Present day, Cushendall, County Antrim, Ireland

A sudden downpour falls through bright sunshine that April afternoon when I arrive in the sleepy village of Cushendall in County Antrim. As the iron key turns to open the heavy door, the old tower leans and creaks hello. The fat spiders twirl in their spinning webs down in the dungeon. The raven winks from the rafters. The spirits stir and flicker.

The caretaker is a butcher. He has left a letter on the kitchen table, a leaflet that is a potted history of the village and the tower and instructions for how to switch the water on and off. It is all so welcoming and friendly:

Welcome to the Curfew Tower
This tower was built in the 1800s
It was built as a prison to keep riotous people,

now it is a haven for artists and writers,
another kind of riotous people altogether
You'll be safe to stay in here
Call me if you need anything,
you'll find me in the butcher's and
my number is here . . .

But the cold door key is in my cold hand and the shape is cold and the feeling is cold and I am thinking about the key and the door and the cold. Am I safe now? Safe from what? Safe in the tower. Am I imprisoned? Isolated? Or protected in a fortress? What is this and which is it? Can it be neither? Can it be both?

I look at the key, big and cold, and tears spring to my eyes. My eyes see things all blurry. Is this real? Was any of it real? The key feels real. The walls, the cold old walls. Yes, the thick and sturdy walls of this tower feel real. Why am I here? Am I being punished? For what? No. Not at all. This will be home for a while, I guess. Wait! I cannot just leave myself in here . . . Hang on, this cannot be right? What will I do in here on my own? Be calm. All I have to do is stay here in the tower now and read and write and have a little think . . . The Desk? How can I finish this book without The Desk? How will I write this without The Desk? These stories were always inside you, inside me, inside here. And not inside The Desk? No. Not inside The Desk, inside my own head. Tears are welling up in my eyes.

One long silent moment. I have a slow realisation. Not The Desk? Not The Desk? Just the desk, a desk? What are you saying? So, does that mean . . . I am alone? Am I alone?

Was I always alone?
I think I am alone.
Alone with my own head.

Oh it's so quiet and empty inside here now. I mumble to the empty kitchen. *What am I going to do with my own self alone in here?* I sit at the table. A twiddle of the thumbs. *Now what? Well? Are you just going to sit there in your coat at the kitchen table? Come on, Wolfie,* I say to myself, *make your mind up, are you coming or going? Are you staying in or going back outside?*

I glance around and find the kitchen is homely. There are tins of tomatoes and beans, bags of pasta and rice. Look where I sit, now this will be a good sturdy kitchen table to write at in the mornings while I have my breakfast. I knock on the kitchen table as you might a door. I knock *a-rat-a-tat,* yes, that is a good table for writing, isn't it? And there is tea! Look! I get up and walk over to the sink and fill the kettle to make tea. Nice tea. Tea makes the world all alright again. Oh shit. I sound like my grandmother. The sound of the kettle click, the sound of the teaspoon in the cup, the sound of the dripping tap, the gurgling of the water in the kettle, these new sounds. This is home for now, just for a while. Outside the barred kitchen window there is a robin in a pot of lavender in the garden. The old window rattles with the wind. I read somewhere that the robin is a symbol of spirits passed, that they carry comfort and messages from the dead. These pretty red-breasted birds often appear to people when they are grieving, when people are in mourning they come to bring comfort. Well, look, here is your robin, Wolf. I start to cry again, it's a strange cry, like a child cries when it is overtired with a scrunched-up nose. I don't even know why I cry, a feeling, a stone in the chest, the weight of it makes me cry.

Has Mrs Death gone now?
Has Mrs Death left me?
Where did she go?
Will she be back?
I don't know any more. I miss her so much.
I miss Mrs Death, does Mrs Death miss me?

When tea is made I leave the kitchen and walk along the corridor and towards the first set of narrow and winding stairs. There is a raven above the dungeon door and I say *kraa-kraa-kraa*. The raven isn't real, or is it? The dungeon door is open, a black mouth, an alarming gaping darkness. I walk into the dungeon. It is cold. I sit in the gloom and drink my tea for a while. I have put myself in prison.

My first thought: who has been here before?

If you sit in a prison, you think, who was here before me? Were they innocent? Were they guilty? Did they die in here? Were they changed and reborn? Did they walk out of here a new person? Who decides how long they stay in here? And what is law and what is wrong and right and what is guilt and what is innocence? Who decides who is imprisoned and who is free? Who keeps the key and keeps us captive? Do we imprison our own selves? Like me right now sitting in this dungeon and sitting in a cage in my head. I sniff. It smells dusty in here. What is the meaning of freedom? Who is truly free? I ponder on all of this for a long while, sipping my tea, and the tears that fell have dried on my cheeks.

I leave the dungeon to walk along the corridor and climb the narrow wooden stairs. The steps creak with each step. The tower is strong and square, a window on each side. I gaze down and out of the four windows. I look north, south, east and west; I can see everything from up here, I feel like I am in a lighthouse. I peer at books on the shelves and art and paintings left by the last visitors here. I look around the room and think about setting up a good place to do some writing. There is a green desk by the easterly window that'll do nicely. But then I decide to go for a walk to see the sea and check out the beach. I decide to write a poem on the tongue and to record it, looking out at the sea and the sky. I lock the door and leave the tower. The fat robin stares from the lavender. I nod to the robin, *We will be friends,* I tell it, *don't you worry, I will feed you toast crusts every morning.* The robin makes as though it has heard and understood, it nods and hops along the wall before perching back in the lavender. I pull the old creaky gate to and head down towards the beach.

Outside and walking I go: Left leg, right leg, one foot in front of the other.

It is a windy afternoon, above me a hazy sky and a taste of salt. There's nobody around, not really, it's dead, dead quiet. I walk and listen to the world, to birds, to seagulls and a distant crashing of waves. I walk down the lane and towards the sea. Take it all in. Breathing in and exhaling, in and out, whilst watching the froth and crash of waves. This is a magic place, the colours are beautiful, the sage, viridescent sea and pale lilac skies, with a shock of yellow gorse on the cliffs and banks. I keep walking and take the high road up the cliff path, up and up and upwards to get a panoramic view, higher and higher, up and upwards towards the church ruins. Slippery. Be careful. Should have worn boots . . . yes, but I don't own any boots. It is all very well saying should've worn boots when even I know I don't even own any boots even, even . . .

I walk slowly, take it easy, stopping once or twice to look back down at the bay of Cushendall beach. So still, so peaceful. I gaze ahead and out to sea. In the far-off distance one can just about make out the Mull of Kintyre. I reach a peak, a curve in the cliff face. I sit on the edge, on the soft green grass, the lush and new springy grass. I need a smoke. I look for a cigarette, something to smoke, did I bring smokes? Do I have any tobacco left? I cannot remember. I feel in my jacket pockets, ripped pockets, the pockets of the jacket lining are destroyed, my things get lost inside the jacket lining fabric, I tut, and no, and then, hang on, maybe in my jeans, jean pockets, something, and there is something and it is then I find the locket, that silver locket. The silver locket with a rabbit engraved on the front. I put it on, I feel it around my throat. Ha! So there is some proof it was real, it is real. I am real!

Tilly Tuppence, she was real. Martha and Marsha, they were real. They are all in me. It was ALL me and it is real. The desk is real. Mrs Death is real. Not a dream. And not a manifestation, not a hallucination, but a real, real, real, real . . . memory.

Mrs Death, can you hear me? You were real! We were real! Mrs Death, are you going to talk to me? We were all here, all of us live inside me here, all of us live always!

My feet dangle. Rocks. Jagged. Rocks.

There is nothing but miles of air and the thundering waves below me. The water is smashing and crashing at the sharp rocks, miles beneath my feet. A strong sea wind picks up and whips the vivid yellow gorse bushes that line the rough cliff face. My hair is wild and in my face; it's getting in my mouth. There are thick prickly hedges and the deep sea froths and crashes to rocks below.

I could jump now.
Unwanted thought.
Is that what you want?
Jump.
Unwanted thought.
No.
That was an unwanted thought.
Just one wrong foot.
Unwanted thought.
Just lean forwards.
Just let go.
Give up!
I imagine it.
Wolf. Imagine it.

I imagine falling. Vividly. Why? Just imagine it. Why? Look down. Vertigo. Stomach flips. I feel dizzy. I see the rocks. I see coloured spots. What kills you? What would kill me first? The rocks, the water, the current, the fall, the shock, the cold, the tide, the sharks? Which would kill me? Would it be the rock smashing my head open or the waves dragging me under? Drowning is a beautiful death, isn't that what everyone says? What if I misjudged it? What if I didn't even hit the water and landed all crooked there, on those rocks and gorse bushes? What if I landed on the rock and broke my back and had to lie there as eagles swooped down and feasted, picked at my eyes and ate out my liver and kidneys? What if I lived only to be drowned a few hours later as the tide came in and pulled me away under the waves? And what if they never found my body, like my father? What if I leave my clothes, folded neat, so it looks like I dived in, like a mistake, like I'm a healthy joyful person who likes swimming? They would find my phone and shoes and know I am vanished. I imagine that too much. I could do that, I could fall and I could disappear under the surface like my father.

Listen to the ocean. Listen to the water. The ocean never changes her mind, the ocean, she says what she wants to say. Today we shall say what we mean to say. Say what we mean to say. Say it.

I know a lot of living people now.

I hear a voice:

I know a lot of living people now.

She speaks to me:

I know a lot of living people now. And I know living is inevitable and necessary. Without breathing you wouldn't live; without knowing you breathe this would be endless. That is why you need to breathe. Without breath this would be a never-ending conveyor belt of sensation. You would be nothing without living in your breath. So breathe. Take five deep breaths. Breathe. Breathe. Breathe. Breathe.

Breathe. To imagine your own life is to be living. To be friends, to be friendly with the knowledge, the knowing that living is now, this should make you try harder to be living, to be fully alive and lively. Surely you know you are alive? You know, you all know, that you're here and now and only here and now? This should make you want to be good, to be better. You know, since you are here and shit, you may as well give a shit.

To imagine your own life is to imagine that this is all. To visualise the life of your elders, your parents, your siblings, your children, your lover, your world, to imagine these loving lives should make you try harder. In theory. It should make you try hard to be a better person. What a glorious mess this living is. And you can call me Life.

Have we met before?

I'm not sure we have, Wolf.

Are you Life?

Yes. Are you alive?

Who, me?

Yes, you. Yes or no? It's a very simple question I ask. Walk with me, come and walk with Life. I am Life and I am here to be with you. I am I. I am me. I am you and you are alive. I am your Life.

Smell that sea salt on the air. Remember salt is in everything. Take everything with a pinch of salt. Open the windows in your head and let the light in. Let the light in your head pour into your beating heart. Can you feel me? Come with me, Wolf. Walk one step at a time. It is your turn now. This is your life, your one precious life, it is your time to walk with Life, this is your time, time for the time of your Life.

And the light of your Life, I can see it, it is here inside you, you have so much Life ahead of you.

So, it's an easy choice, yes or no, is it yes or no? Do you want to walk with the living, to really live your one Life or will you continue to pretend to live? Do you live a lie or do you live your truth? Think about it, take your time, take all the time you need, take one day at a time. Do your lifetime in your own lifetime.

It's a very simple question that Life asks: *Will you walk with me?*

Wolf's Tower Diaries

Ireland, April 2018

April 1st

I walk along
a cliff path
sea salt and
yellow gorse
I'm on my own
and
I don't know
where this path
will lead
but
I am here
and
here
I am

April 2nd

At night
the tower
comes to life
the walls talk
a fear
consumes me
my heart is loud
dum-dum
dum-dum
no sign of
Mrs Death
it's dead quiet
I miss Death

April 3rd

In the village
the florist
sells sad tulips
and candles
of St Francis
I tell her
I stay in the tower
the look of dread
on her face is priceless
she shakes her head and
forewarns me
666 is written in Layd

April 4th

Fear of solitude
fear of the dark
fear of the unknown
fear of the dead
fear is in my head
tricks of the mind
tricks of light and shadow
the heart is a mimic
boom boom boom
the heart goes
thumping like a rabbit's foot
but there's nothing there
nothing but your own fear

April 5th

The butcher
sells me
five sausages
and an onion
as big as my face
he knows
I stay in the tower
the look of joy
on his face is priceless
he smiles his big smiles
have you been to Layd
666 is written in Layd

April 6th

In the village
I go to the library
and read the
local newspaper

Thirty years to this day
when she was last seen alive
the police say they
have fresh leads

What happened to Inga
the girl
they found
in the woods

April 7th

I climb the path
to visit Layd
old church ruins
and a graveyard
high on the cliff top
beautiful view
I'm roaring
and it rains
and it pours

April 8th

The china rabbit
sits on my desk
I can do this
I slept well
last night
no nightmares
my feeling today
I can do this
my own heart says
live, live, live
I am alive in here
says the rabbit

April 9th

The fire is my friend
glowing there
in the corner of the room
when the fire is
roaring and crackling
I am not alone at all
I talk to the fire
I am good at keeping
the fire going
the conversation
with fire burning

April 10th

Today I wrote about people vanishing
I wrote about disappearances
as I walked down a sea path
that led to nowhere
the destination
vanished off
a cliff edge

April 11th

Time and Death are lovers
Life will not concern herself
with the romance
between Time and Death
Life loves a good Time
Time is an unfaithful lover
Time be just like my father
Death be just like my mother

April 12th

Sometimes
I think I can do this
I fetch the coal or
I make tea
then a light bulb blows
and I am lost
in the dark
again

April 13th

I don't know why
I put the china rabbit
in my suitcase and
brought her to Ireland
I sit her on this table
looking at me
as I write this
there are things
that we hold on to
we hold on tightly
time can pass
and years go by
and these things
and these objects
and these people
and these ideas
that we held so tightly

we have to let them go
we hold them in
hold them down to be
who we think they are
what we want them to be
and what they mean to us
and holding on to people
like old ideas and bad habits
or like china rabbits
now we don't need to be
doing that now
do we

April 14th

The tower is an old lady
and she is full of wind
she keeps popping her head in
with draughts and spiders
I try to be polite and listen
she'll let you know
you're in her home
she makes her walls
groan at three a.m.
here is the murder hole
here's the dungeon
here's a ghost
yes, I know
but I'm
trying
to sleep

April 15th

I go to Ballypatrick forest
where they found Inga
I picture her running
through the bluebells
through the woods
through the trees
running for
Life

April 16th

I thought it was a good idea
to live in a tower
with spiders and shadows
and write about Death
but the more I write this book
the more I see the chinks
of light and humour
Death is not
locked up in a tower
she is dancing
on the beach
salt and sea spray
in the bluebells and woods
the yellow moss-covered rocks
the patches of blue
above the green
open sea

April 17th

In the village pub
there is a man
called Seamus
he says he loves
Dwight Yoakam
but nobody else in
Cushendall does
he laughs
he says he thinks he can sing
like Dwight Yoakam
but nobody else in
Cushendall thinks he can

April 18th

We dance around
a talk of Death
there are so
many words
so many ways
to avoid it
passed
passed over
passed away
what is this
odd language
we use around
Death?
these words
we hide behind?
she is dead
he is dead

I am mourning
I say it to myself
they died
so I must
be mourning
say what has happened
use the language
the words you know
we often hide behind words
we often say nothing at all

April 19th

The dead of night
the tower screams
give up give up give up
it shakes with the wind
thunder and lightning
the walls vibrate
the windows rattle
the fire dies
all is cold and
I do not sleep
then dawn breaks
I am thankful for first light
I put on my coat and walk
and walk and walk and walk
higher and higher and higher
I am high up on the cliffs
overlooking the ocean

watching the sun rise
listening to birdsong
I am real
I am alive
I am grateful
for every
breath

April 20th

The weather
is mad
blue sky rain
grey sky
sunshine
storms
the sea is
razors and
feathers

April 21st

I fall sleep
my hair all in knots
lips taste of sea salt
nails ripped and
black with coal dust
I blow smoke
and talk fluent fire

April 22nd

I am not alone
I stare into the flames
and talk to the fire
I am good at keeping
the fire going
and this conversation
with the fire burns forever

April 23rd

Nothing lasts
Nothing is finished
Nothing is perfect

Death lasts
Death isn't finished
Death is perfect

Life lasts
Life isn't finished
Life is perfect

Love lasts
Love isn't finished
Love is perfect

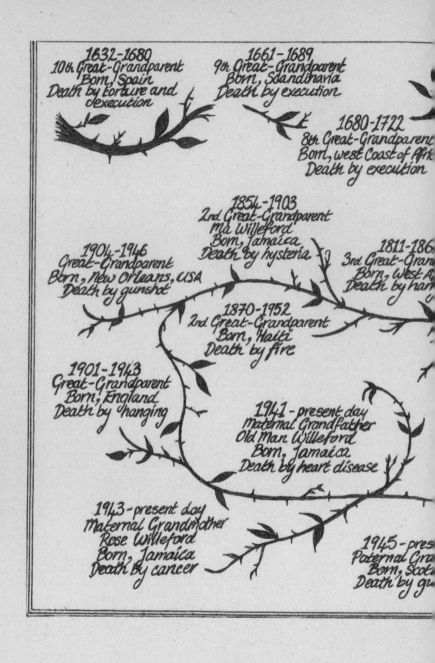

1632–1680
10th Great-Grandparent
Born, Spain
Death by torture and
execution

1661–1689
9th Great-Grandparent
Born, Scandinavia
Death by execution

1680–1722
8th Great-Grandparent
Born, west Coast of Afri
Death by execution

1854–1903
2nd Great-Grandparent
Ma Willeford
Born, Jamaica
Death by hysteria

1904–1946
Great-Grandparent
Born, New Orleans, USA
Death by gunshot

1811–186
3rd Great-Gran
Born, West A
Death by han

1870–1952
2nd Great-Grandparent
Born, Haiti
Death by fire

1901–1943
Great-Grandparent
Born, England
Death by hanging

1941 – present day
Maternal Grandfather
Old Man Willeford
Born, Jamaica
Death by heart disease

1943 – present day
Maternal Grandmother
Rose Willeford
Born, Jamaica
Death by cancer

1945 – pres
Paternal Gra
Born, Scot
Death by gu

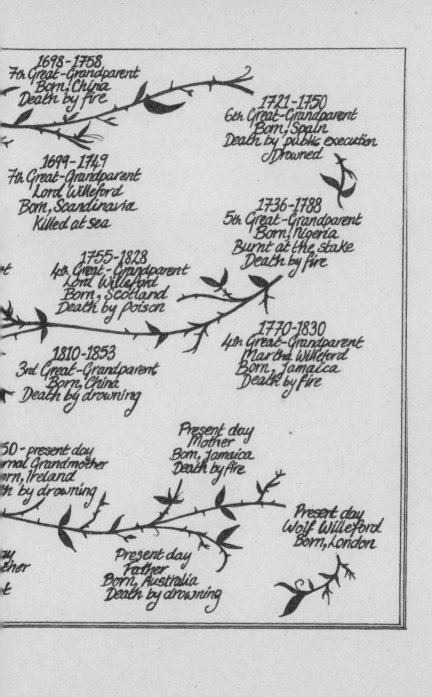

1698-1758
7th Great-Grandparent
Born, China
Death by fire

1721-1750
6th Great-Grandparent
Born, Spain
Death by public execution
Drowned

1699-1749
7th Great-Grandparent
Lord Willeford
Born, Scandinavia
Killed at sea

1736-1788
5th Great-Grandparent
Born, Nigeria
Burnt at the stake
Death by fire

1755-1828
4th Great-Grandparent
Lord Willeford
Born, Scotland
Death by poison

1770-1830
4th Great-Grandparent
Martha Willeford
Born, Jamaica
Death by fire

1810-1853
3rd Great-Grandparent
Born, China
Death by drowning

Present day
Mother
Born, Jamaica
Death by fire

50 - present day
rnal Grandmother
orn, Ireland
h by drowning

Present day
Wolf Willeford
Born, London

Present day
Father
Born, Australia
Death by drowning

Wolf's Timeline:

1632–1680	10th great-grandparent, born Spain, death by torture and execution
1661–1689	9th great-grandparent, born Scandinavia, death by execution
1680–1722	8th great-grandparent, born west cost of Africa, death by execution
1698–1758	7th great-grandparent, born Congo, death by fire
1699–1749	7th great-grandparent, Lord Willeford, born Scandinavia, killed at sea
1721–1750	6th great-grandparent, born Spain, witch, public execution, drowned
1736–1788	5th great-grandparent, born Nigeria, witch, burnt at stake, death by fire
1755–1828	4th great-grandparent, Lord Willeford, born Scotland, death by poison
1770–1830	4th great-grandparent, Martha Willeford, born Jamaica, death by fire

1810–1853	3rd great-grandparent, born China, died by drowning
1811–1861	3rd great-grandparent, born West Africa, died by hanging
1854–1903	2nd great-grandparent, Ma Willeford, born Jamaica, death by hysteria
1870–1952	2nd great-grandparent, born Haiti, died by fire
1904–1946	1st great-grandparent, born New Orleans, USA, died by gunshot
1901–1943	1st great-grandparent, born England, name unknown, death by hanging
1941–present day	Wolf's mother's father, Old Man Willeford, born Jamaica, death by heart disease
1943–present day	Wolf's mother's mother, Rose Willeford, born Jamaica, death by cancer
1945–present day	Wolf's father's father, born Scotland, death by gunshot
1950–present day	Wolf's father's mother, born Ireland, death by drowning
Present day	Wolf's mother, born Jamaica, death by fire
Present day	Wolf's father, born Australia, death by drowning
Present day	Wolf Willeford, born London

Thank You . . .

To my forever love Richard. To my mum and mum, my brothers and sisters, my nieces and nephews and all our beautiful family. To our grandparents, may they rest in peace. To our ancestors who echo in these pages. To you who shaped my words until I was compelled to write this. To our father, Paul: rest in peace, Dad.

To my agent, Crystal Mahey-Morgan, Jason Morgan, Shae Davis and the brilliant OWN IT! family. Thank you to my editor, Hannah Knowles. Thanks also to Anna Frame, Lucy Zhou, Aa'Ishah Hawton, Leila Cruickshank, Vicki Rutherford, Joanna Lord, Katalina Watt, Kate Oliver, Vicki Watson, Jenny Fry, Francis Bickmore, Jamie Byng and everyone in the fabulous Canongate team.

I'm indebted to all deceased mentioned in this book. With love and respect, we salute you and remember you here. Rest in peace. Rest in power. Here's to the families of thousands of black and working class and vulnerable people, key workers, carers and nurses, that we lost to Covid-19 due to the ineptitude of those who still continue to put profit before life.

To the spirit that first whispered to me on Brick Lane and on the beach of Koh Kood, where the first pages were written. Thank you to the ghosts who called to me on the Causeway Coast and Glen where the last pages were written. To Bill Drummond, the Neu! Reekie! Crew, the Curfew Tower and all the kind folk of Cushendall.

Thanks to The Society of Authors, The Royal Literary Fund and The Royal Society of Literature. To the BBC and Cecile Wright for producing the Radio 4 documentary of this work in progress. To composer Peter Coyte, who collaborated with me to co-write Mrs Death's songs.

To all friends and family of Churchtown, F23 and Cosmic Trigger. Thanks to the Book of Horkos and special mention to dear Claudia The Mighty.

I have been given lots of guidance along the way, life-changing advice and inspiration. Thank you for your friendship, your work, your generosity, your art, books and music; thank you to all poets, authors, activists and artists.

Thanks to you, dear reader, to all the people who've shared my work and shown support online and in real life. Thanks to all bookshops, libraries and book bloggers. Thanks to all death workers, death doula, the death positive movement and all who continue to encourage this open conversation. Thanks to all who remind me to keep fighting the good fight. Thank you for your wisdom and your hope. Thank you to all who listened and laughed with me in the kitchen, with a rum in hand, watching the sunrise.

Rabbit: The Last Words

We end this book with a silent salute and leave six blank pages.

We leave these pages blank as a silent memorial for all the names we do not know and cannot say. For all the invisible, the undervalued, the unmarked and the unresolved. For all that is becoming extinct, a blank page for the bleached coral reef, depleted rainforests, dead rivers and obsolete wildlife. The last elephant.

We leave these pages blank for all we are losing and have lost to the coronavirus pandemic. To all drowned souls in unmarked watery graves. These empty pages are a salute to all the murdered, the disappeared, the stolen and the erased. The fallen and the pushed. May their light be remembered here.

In the beginning of this work, in the Disclaimer, Wolf Willeford wrote: *This book does not mention every person that has ever died — if you wished this book to have mentioned another death, we can only apologise now in advance, for not knowing which death you wanted celebrated in this book . . .*

Together you and I can address this: now I ask you to write the name that came to your mind as you read this story. Please add your loved one's name on one of these blank pages, maybe add a date, a memory or a prayer. In this one act of remembrance we will be united. From now on every single person who reads this book will know their copy contains their own dead. As time passes, if this book is borrowed or passed along, the names will live on. This will be universal and timeless. This is our private ritual.

Now this book contains not just the dead Wolf may know of and that Mrs Death may mention, but the names each of you may want to remember here today. And in the future anyone who reads your copy of this book will read that handwritten name and speak it aloud.

One day they may read your own name. One day they may read mine. In this we are connected. We share these names of our loved ones in the whisper of the last page turning, over the years to come.